"We showed that we are united
and that we, young people,
are unstoppable."

—GRETA THUNBERG,
UN Youth Climate Summit,
New York City, 21 September 2019

For all the rebels ...
just keep going.

CHAPTER One

"Effie! Effie! Effie!"

The crowd chants my name as I ascend to the podium, waving my hand with a tiny twist of the wrist like the Queen. I look out at the crowd, smile, then lean forward to speak into the microphone. There is a screech of feedback and then silence, as if all the people in front of me are holding their breath. When I speak, my voice rings out firm and strong.

"My fellow citizens," I say. "We stand together today shoulder to shoulder in the fight against climate change. I am thrilled to announce the official rolling out of the new green policy that I have introduced with the help of my close personal friends Michelle Obama and Greta Thunberg. I pledge that this victory is the first of many – a victory for fairness, a victory for equality, a victory for the environment, and above all –" I pause "– above all, a victory for HOPE!"

The crowd erupts once more, cheering and shouting my name.

"Effie! Effie!"

"Effie! I cannot believe you're making us hike up this actual mountain." Kevin huffs, cutting through my beautiful daydream as sharply as a pair of ceremonial ribbon-cutting scissors. His cheeks are almost as red as the woolly hat he's wearing.

"It's hardly a mountain, Kev," I say, returning to the real world. "It's really more of a gentle incline."

"What sort of gentle incline takes twenty minutes to climb? This is a mountain."

"A mountain is classified as being over a thousand feet high," Jess chimes in. Jess is very literal and she keep us all honest about things.

The way Zo is glaring at me from deep inside her big duffel coat makes it clear she's not exactly on my side here. Zo is a girl of few words. She was badly bullied at her last school and it's taken her a long time to relax around us. But her glare is really speaking . . . she can say a lot without actually *saying* a lot.

"Yeah, but *why*?" Ruby asks, with an extravagant

groan. Ruby is just about the coolest girl in the year above and a real force to be reckoned with. "Why are we doing this? We can hardly have a picnic anyway, it's FREEZING."

I suppose she does have a point there. It may be March but it's very, very cold. I've recently started to wonder if we are stuck in a never-ending winter, like we've accidentally journeyed into Narnia or something. (I could just fancy some Turkish delight, actually, and I'd definitely make a benevolent queen and leader. Plus, I reckon I'd be quite handy with a sword.) Maybe I *had* been a touch optimistic when I suggested we all go for a walk and a picnic as a nice Sunday afternoon activity. But optimism is practically my middle name, and anyway I'm not going to apologize for getting us all out in the fresh air and beautiful nature.

"Well, I think it's nice to be outside," Angelika pipes up, like the true best friend and kindred spirit that she is. I grin at her. I knew she'd understand – sometimes it's like the two of us share a brain. We just get each other.

The six of us met when we ran a frankly outstanding political campaign against my one-time personal nemesis/now sort-of friend, Aaron Davis, before Christmas. I narrowly lost the race for student council president at my new school, and as someone with an awful lot of political ambition I have to admit that this taste of defeat was BITTER INDEED. It took me a while to bounce back from it. Sometimes it still makes me a bit sad if I think about it, and my confidence is not quite what it once was (although I did have ever such a lot to start with). Luckily, I have my amazing campaign team to keep my spirits high.

Over the past few months we six have formed an unshakeable and deep bond, the kind that soldiers make when they've been into battle together. I'd do anything for this lot, and I know they feel the same about me. Having friends like that makes me extremely lucky, especially because moving to a new school a few weeks into year eight was lonely at first.

Sometimes it takes you a while to find your people.

"Come on, guys," I say encouragingly now, rallying the troops with my trademark enthusiasm. "It will all be worth it in the end. This spot down by the river is magic. It's like something out of a story."

This statement is greeted by a stony silence. I know they're going to love it once they see it though. There's a grassy bank that slopes gently down to the blue water, perfect for picnicking and making daisy chains. Weeping willow trees dip their graceful branches into the river and kingfishers zip along the surface, dazzling blurs of electric blue. There are fluffy ducklings to feed and a little stone bridge where you can play Poohsticks (the game invented by Winnie-the-Pooh, where you choose sticks and race them through the water).

"I bought hot chocolate. And biscuits." I jiggle my backpack. "Hobnobs."

"*Chocolate* Hobnobs?" Kevin asks.

"Of course, I'm not a monster."

Everyone perks up, just like I knew they would. Sometimes being a good leader is about keeping morale high in difficult circumstances, and I have found that hot chocolate and biscuits are a pretty sure-fire morale booster. Maybe I should write to the prime minister with this kind of wisdom. Sometimes I think world leaders just don't get how MUCH people like chocolate.

Soon we start heading downhill and the mood improves even more.

We chat about what we watched on telly last night, and the ferocious maths homework, and Kevin's mum's latest health kick and the monstrosities he's had to eat. ("There's suddenly so much cabbage," he says, shuddering.) It's nice, the chatter and the laughing. Relaxed. Easy.

"Almost there!" I exclaim as we wind our way through a shady wood. It's the sort of place where you wouldn't be surprised to find fairies or woodland spirits. The light coming through the trees is smudgy and gold.

We round a corner and the river opens out in front of us. And I come to a screeching halt.

"Wh-wh-what?" I gasp.

I have rather unhelpfully frozen in the middle of the path. The others peer out from behind me.

The sight that greets me makes my heart squeeze in my chest. The graceful willows are tangled up with plastic bags. There are no ducklings, no kingfishers. Just a river choked with rubbish – plastic bottles, crisp packets, fast food wrappers, trapped in greasy brown water.

I stumble down the bank and crane my neck to see down to the river bend. Litter everywhere, as far as I can see.

"What is going on?" I say.

"Something must have happened upstream," Ruby says. "This is a crazy amount of litter."

"It's terrible," Angelika breathes.

"Horrible," Kevin says, trying to fish a carrier bag out of the water with a stick.

"Somebody should do something," Jess says.

Her words are a wake-up call, cutting through the fog in my brain.

"Oh, somebody WILL do something," I say fiercely, spinning around. I look at the dynamic team huddled before me. A grim smile tugs at my lips and I feel adrenaline pump through my veins. "And it's going to be us."

CHAPTER Two

Back at home that evening I am staring at my history homework while I sit at the kitchen table. The image of the poor river is stuck in my brain as if it's been superglued there and I'm finding it hard to concentrate.

"Effie! You left your shoes in my meditation space again!" my sister Lil's voice shrills. "How many times must I tell you?! It is IMPOSSIBLE for me to achieve a sense of SERENITY when your mess is everywhere."

Lil is eight. She may look cute, but she is most generously described as "a bit of a handful" and more often as "an evil genius". In a bid for general calm, I recently encouraged her to take up mindfulness meditation. The results have been mixed.

"You are much messier than me," I sigh, moving through to the darkened living room, where she sits cross-legged on the floor, staring pointedly at the single trainer that lies in front of her. I move the shoe slightly to one side.

Lil rolls her eyes at me. "My *mess*, as you call it, is merely another sign of my creative spirit."

Mum and Dad wouldn't let Lil have a candle because of the fire risk (Lil was outraged and railed against such a blatantly ageist decision with a passion that I actually found quite stirring) so her "meditation space" consists of an old torch that she stands upright on the carpet and an old CD of whale song that she found in the garage.

"You look stressed, Effie. Come. Sit with me," she

says invitingly, her voice pitched to a more soothing level. It's worth a shot, I suppose. I sit beside her and cross my legs. "Now, let's do some breathing exercises. Breathe in ... breathe out. Breathe in ... breathe out."

As the minutes pass, I realize that I haven't really given meditation a fair chance before. All this slow breathing is quite soothing. I even like the whale song. I feel my limbs start to relax.

I keep my mind clear and concentrate only on my breathing. Innnnnn ... and outtttttt. Innnnnn ... and outtttttttt. Innn...

I blink as suddenly the torch begins to flash quickly, with a strobe-like effect.

"It's just Dad's old torch." Lil's voice remains even. "Every so often it starts flashing the SOS code. It'll stop in a minute."

So much for relaxation. The torch is LITERALLY flashing a massive distress signal all over the room. I feel my shoulders tensing back up.

There's a tap on the window and I rush over to open it.

"Are you girls having a rave in there?" a voice croaks. "Shall I go and get my glow sticks?"

Our neighbour Iris is outside in her wheelchair.

She sticks her head through the window to have a good look. Iris is over ninety years old, she has bright pink hair, and she's just about the coolest person I know. She's also one of the grumpiest.

"What's this music? I don't understand the appeal at all. In my day, music had . . ." She gestures widely with her arms as the whale song reaches an echoey crescendo. ". . . a bit of a tune at least."

"Hello, Iris!" I say. "We're just doing a bit of quiet meditation." I press pause on the CD and the whales stop mid-groan. "No rave here, I'm afraid."

"Oh," Iris says, looking a bit disappointed.

"Oh, hello, Iris," Dad says as he comes into the room. "Are you coming in for a cuppa? I baked revani today."

"There's revani?" Lil leaps to her feet. "Why was I not told about this earlier?" She almost mows Dad down on her sprint to the kitchen.

"Don't eat it all," Dad calls. "You know your mum will be starving when she gets in from the library."

Mum is a lecturer at the local uni and she spends an awful lot of time in the library, fighting with a poet who has been dead for eight hundred years. It is hungry work.

"HANG ON. WHERE'S MY CHOCOLATE MILK?"

Lil's voice thunders.

Dad gives me a terrified look. "I knew I forgot something at the supermarket!" he whispers.

I draw a single finger slowly across my neck.

"Oho! You're dead meat!" Iris chuckles fondly. She has a soft spot for Lil.

"Maybe she'll be distracted by the cake," I say optimistically. Revani is a Greek cake made with semolina and a shed-load of syrup and it tastes A-MAZING. My yia-yia taught Dad how to make it, and as distractions go it is up there with the best of them.

"Mmm." Dad doesn't look convinced. "Fancy coming in, Iris? You can protect me."

"Can't today," Iris says. "I haven't got time for socializing. There are important letters to write. These politicians think we're all idiots, but I'll show them."

"In that case, let me get you a slice to take with you," Dad says, and goes off to the kitchen.

Iris is always on a letter-writing campaign. In fact, Iris and I first bonded over our shared determination to make a difference. Iris has spent her whole life protesting and campaigning, which makes her a proper, real-life hero.

Recently, we've been talking a lot about the environment and what we can do to make a change. It was one of the issues that I wanted to tackle if I got elected to school council. I guess that's all at an end now – and seeing the state of the river has only brought up all my feelings of frustration again.

"I know that look." Iris gives me a beady stare. "You're thinking about the election again. Moping."

"I'm not moping," I say quickly. "Well, maybe a bit. I was just going to make so many changes, and now I can't."

"There's more than one way to change things," Iris says, rolling back her wheelchair to fix me with her sharp gaze. "You're going to let a little thing like losing one election stop you, are you?" Dad reappears with her cake wrapped in tinfoil. "Thank you very much. Come round soon, Effie."

I stand for a moment watching her make her way up the garden path. Iris is right. I don't need to be student council president to make a difference. There are other ways I can change things. After all, some of my biggest heroes are the rebels – look at Malala Yousafzai or Autumn Peltier or Ellen Jones. They aren't in charge, but they make their voices heard. They CHANGE things.

I feel something stirring inside me then, a fighting spirit that has been quiet for too long. I am still Effie Kostas, after all. I can still make change happen . . . and I know just the team to help me do it.

CHAPTER *Three*

Even though it has been almost three months since I lost the election, my friends and I still like to meet up from time to time in our campaign office. (Some with less vision might call it a store cupboard, but they'd be mistaken.)

It's more than a campaign office to us now. It's OUR space, our sanctuary, our mission control centre. The walls of the office are covered in bright pictures and posters – mostly drawn by our resident artist, Kevin – and there are big purple cushions on the floor. The shelves are stacked neatly with dazzling tubes of (environmentally friendly) glitter glue, crisp sheets of (recycled) paper in all different colours, and a collection of marker pens that ranges from sparkly to scented. In short, it is every stationery fan's dream, and another highly successful collaboration between me and Angelika.

Watching the gang now, sprawled on the cushions, arguing about who is the superior Marvel hero, with the electric bulb humming overhead, I feel so happy. This room feels warm and friendly and full of possibility.

"Right," I say, interrupting the Captain Marvel versus Thor face-off. "I need to talk to you lot about something important."

"This IS important," Ruby huffs, shaking her head and making all her long, thin braids swish. "Have you seen Thor's muscles? I rest my case."

"I think Effie has her presidential voice on," Kevin says, sitting up.

"Oooh," Jess says. "Haven't heard that for a while."

"Is this about the river?" Angelika asks keenly.

"Partly," I say. "I realized that sorting out the river is actually just one part of a bigger problem."

"What do you mean?" Ruby scrunches her nose up in confusion.

"Well, we can organize a river clean-up," I say. "But all the litter is coming from somewhere. And one of those places is probably right here. This school." I gesture around us. "We don't even have recycling bins. Now, I know that Aaron has made *some* improvements as student council president. . ."

"He put up that suggestion box." Jess nods. "The one where students can raise issues for the council to discuss. That was a good idea."

"And the weekly pizza," Ruby adds. "I'm not exactly unhappy about that."

"Yes, those were good ideas," I say, fairly. "I still think he can do better. We ran a great campaign based on things we really wanted to change at the school, and we shouldn't give up on those issues just because we didn't win."

"What did you have in mind?" Angelika asks, sitting up straighter. I can already see the gleam in her eyes, the one that I know is a mirror for mine. When I am prime minister one day, I am certain that Angelika will be the campaign manager who gets me there.

"Well," I say, feeling strangely nervous about sharing my idea, "as you know, Aaron and I have called a truce. We're maybe even . . . friends. Ish. It seems to me that he would be open to a suggestion. There's more to being president than pizza."

"Although pizza is pretty good," Ruby points out.

"We all love pizza, Ruby!" I say. "But do you know what tastes better than pizza?" I pause dramatically. "DEMOCRACY."

"I don't think democracy tastes of anything, does it?" Jess asks doubtfully.

"*Metaphorically* it does," I say firmly. "Metaphorically, democracy tastes like . . . like. . ."

"Like vanilla cupcakes with rainbow sprinkles," Angelika jumps in helpfully.

"Or . . . like . . . salt and vinegar crisp sandwiches." Kevin tips his head thoughtfully to one side. "Made with tiger bread."

"Oooooh," Ruby says. "Democracy sounds delicious."

"Yes, yes," I jump in hastily. "Democracy IS delicious, but the point is if our current administration isn't doing enough, it's up to the PEOPLE to change things. And who are we???"

"Um . . . people?" Jess frowns.

"EXACTLY." I begin to pace, which is hard given how small the cupboard is. "It's up to us to challenge things. One of the things on our list of campaign promises was a recycling programme. Given the climate crisis we face, it's criminal that we don't have recycling bins and the canteen is full of water

bottles and plastic packaging." They all nod. "SO . . .
I propose we liaise with Aaron and the council to
make a GREEN DEAL. It would be a totally different
approach to rubbish and recycling at the school,
AND it would include fundraising and organizing
the river clean-up."

"Wow." Kevin looks a bit dazed. "That's . . . a lot."

My heart sinks a little. Is this way too ambitious?
Am I going to look like an idiot if I fail again?

"Well, saving the planet is a pretty big job," I say
in what I hope is a rallying tone.

There's a pause, and I can practically hear all our
brains whirring as we think it over.

"Well, I think it's a really good idea." Zo's voice is
quiet but we all look at her. She tends to speak up
only when it's important.

"I agree," Angelika says.

"It's the right thing to do," Kevin says firmly.
"Where do we start?"

"We can go to Aaron and the council," I reply
quickly, enthusiasm bubbling through me like hot
lava. "I think if I explain things to him he'll be on
our side. Together we can approach the rest of the
students and get them interested, talk to the teachers.
We can organize a fundraiser for the river clean-up.

We'll need to raise some money – we have to make sure anyone who wants to be involved can be. I think we'll need a minibus. . ."

"And equipment," Angelika breaks in. "Litter pickers and gloves."

"Kevin can make some of his brilliant posters," Jess says.

"It's about time this school saw what we can really do." Ruby rubs her hands together.

"For Highworth Grange!" I yell, raising my fist in the air, like I'm a general uniting the troops.

"For Highworth Grange!"

CHAPTER *Four*

The first step in my plan is to have a talk with Aaron, and as luck would have it I run into him in the corridor just after the last lesson of the day.

"Aaron!" I exclaim, seizing his arm. He jumps slightly, and I wonder whether I might have been a bit too enthusiastic. My hair is practically crackling with CAN-DO SPIRIT and it's making it even bigger and wilder than usual. I smooth it down. "Can I talk to you about something?" I ask, more calmly.

"Sure, Kostas. What's up?" Aaron asks, hitching his backpack up on his shoulder.

"Hi, Aaron," a voice comes from behind Aaron, and I notice Katie Thomas, his on-again off-again girlfriend, standing there. "Oh, hi, Effie."

Katie is in my year. Her hair is always smooth and shiny and perfect and when you look at her and Aaron standing next to each other they just sort of … *go*, you know? Like a pair of salt and pepper pots. She can also be pretty mean though, and she doesn't seem to like me very much, which Angelika says demonstrates incredibly poor taste.

"Hi, Katie." I wave, trying my friendliest smile on her.

"PREZ!" Just like that we are interrupted by another, unwelcome voice. Matt Spader. I try not to roll my eyes as he and Aaron engage in an elaborate handshake.

He's another good-looking boy from the year above, all curly golden hair and dimples. He looks like an angel, but nothing could be further from the truth. Matt is Aaron's best friend and student council vice president, and maybe the worst human being in existence. That's not my opinion, it's an actual objective fact. Unfortunately, Aaron can't seem to see that.

What really makes me mad is that Matt LOVES all the perks of being the vice president, but he doesn't want to do any actual work. He thinks he deserves the job, just for *existing*. Sometimes he calls Aaron "Prez" and makes people call him "VP" just to really make sure everyone knows how important they are. Gross.

"Hello, Matt," I say.

"Oh, hi, er . . . Ellie," Matt says, his gaze flickering over me for barely a second.

"It's Effie," I say.

"OK," Matt replies like he's not going to argue with me about what my own name is, which I suppose is generous of him. "Ready for practice, Aaron?"

"Sure thing," Aaron says.

"I need to talk to you for a minute," I say quickly. "It's important."

"If this is another one of your little ideas for the student council, why don't you put it in the suggestion box?" Matt says, fixing me with a dazzling smile that makes him look a bit like an angry crocodile.

"I have put quite a lot of ideas in the suggestion box," I reply. "Not much action seems to have been taken. Anyway, I wasn't talking to you, I was talking to Aaron."

Aaron is grinning. "I've got football practice now, Kostas, but why don't we meet up later?"

"Excellent," I say. I can lobby him properly then. "You could come over to mine afterwards?"

"Cool," Aaron says.

It's only then that I notice Katie and Matt are both staring at us. Clearly, neither of them thought Aaron would acknowledge my existence, and the fact confuses them.

"Catch you later then, Effie," Aaron calls over his shoulder as he walks away. Matt lumbers after him, still looking baffled.

"So you and Aaron are hanging out then?" Katie asks.

"Yes, I need to talk to him about a thing," I say, feeling a bit nervous for some reason. "A school thing."

"You two seem to be getting on better these days," Katie goes on. She's smiling but it's a bit tight, like someone is pulling up the corners of her mouth.

"I guess." I shrug. "I always think it's better being friends with someone than fighting with them. After all, as Abraham Lincoln once said –" I raise my voice dramatically "– *do I not destroy my enemies when I make them my friends?*"

Katie gives me a thoughtful look. "Right," she says. "Well, I'll see you around."

As Katie disappears down the hallway with a swish of perfect hair, I turn my mind to more important issues. Like the fact that I only have a couple of hours before I pitch the Green Deal to Aaron.

This DEFINITELY calls for a new ring binder.

CHAPTER *Five*

"What's this I hear about HE-WHO-SHALL-NOT-BE-NAMED coming round?" Lil asks, stomping into the living room. I'm tidying up so that Aaron and I can discuss strategy.

I might be getting on all right with Aaron these days, but Lil is definitely not over him beating me to president. She says it is a "matter of family honour".

"Aaron's not *that* bad," I say. "He's definitely not a Voldemort. If anything, he's more of a Cedric Diggory. Anyway, I need his help with my new idea for the school. It will be much easier if we all work together." I fluff up the cushions on the sofa.

"Well, he's NOT getting any of the good biscuits," Lil says firmly. "I'm going to have a quick word with

Dad. Make sure we're all on the same page."

The doorbell rings ten minutes later and I push my way past the tangle of coats and wellies that fill our little hallway to open it. Aaron is standing there, wrapped up in his winter coat and a blue scarf.

"Hi!" I say. "Come in." There's a brief moment of scuffling as he adds his winter layers to the pile.

"Do you want a drink?" I ask politely.

"That would be nice, thank you," says Aaron, also clearly on his best behaviour.

We go through to the kitchen, where Dad is sitting at the table doing some work. Lil is standing with her arms folded.

"Hi, Mr Kostas," Aaron says.

"Aaron!" Dad exclaims. Aaron has already won my parents over despite the fact that he bested their eldest child in a game of political chess. "Call me Dimitri, remember."

"You may call *me* Ms Kostas," Lil says icily. "Rich tea biscuit?" she asks, holding out a tin.

"Oh, we can do better than that!" Dad exclaims heartily. "I think we've got some chocolate Hobnobs somewhere."

If looks could kill then there's no doubt Dad would be brutally murdered by the glare Lil shoots him.

Dad ignores her, pouring out two big glasses of squash and assembling a plate of biscuits for us. I grab the glasses. Lil makes a brief and wordless "I'm watching you" gesture at Aaron, pointing first at her eyes and then at him. Aaron flinches, the biscuits rattling against the plate in his hand, and he follows me into the sitting room.

We settle on the sofa and Aaron looks at me expectantly. "So, Kostas. What's going on? You're all . . . squiggly. Got another plan to save the world?"

"Funny you should ask that," I say. I take a deep breath and then launch into my plans for the Green Deal.

"It's awful about the river," Aaron says when I've finished. "But don't you think all this might be a bit ambitious for school council?"

"We NEED to be ambitious!" I cry. "Come on, Aaron. I know you could be doing more as president and so do you."

Aaron is quiet for a moment.

"I've collated a few initial ideas," I say, reaching under the sofa. "They're quite rough, but it should be a good starting point." I place a binder bristling with colourful tab dividers on the sofa beside him.

A grin flickers across Aaron's face. "A few initial

ideas. . ." he says, turning the pages. "Effie, there's a table of contents *and* an index. There are several subcategories for minibus suppliers."

"Well, yes," I say. "I do have certain organizational standards."

Aaron just smiles again, his eyes moving rapidly over the pages. He nods a couple of times.

After what feels like hours I burst out, "Well?! What do you think?"

"I still think maybe one or two of these suggestions are just a smidge ambitious."

"Like what?" I ask crossly.

"Um." Aaron runs his finger down the page he's currently on. "For example. Having David Attenborough speak at assembly, followed by a performance by Beyoncé?"

"Oh." I'd actually forgotten I put that in there; I must have been having a revani-based sugar rush. "Well, it's good to aim high."

"It is," Aaron agrees. "But I think we should start with recycling bins, the composting and the school vegetable patch."

"Really?" I beam.

"Yeah." Aaron nods slowly. "It's a brilliant plan, Effie. We can raise it at the council meeting tomorrow and then speak to the head."

"The fundraising priority is the river clean-up. We need transportation and equipment." I flick to the section in the binder dedicated to my research. "It needs to be accessible so that anyone who wants to can be involved. We'll need to sign up lots of volunteers." I frown. "It's a big job."

"That's why the whole Green Deal idea is so good," Aaron says. It seems like my own enthusiasm is contagious. "Because we won't just be cleaning up the river, we'll be tackling the problem at the source by helping everyone at school to be more green."

"Exactly!" I exclaim. "I think we should aim to do the clean-up on the first weekend of the Easter holidays. That way we've got the rest of term to fundraise and spread the word."

"It's the school fete next week," Aaron says thoughtfully. "We could have a stand. Raise money AND sign up volunteers."

"Yes!" I exclaim, almost knocking the plate of biscuits over. "That's a great idea!"

A flush rises in Aaron's cheeks. "Really?" he says.

I nod eagerly. "And we don't have to stop there," I say, the ideas tumbling over themselves in my brain, so fast my mouth can hardly keep up. "We can make the whole fete a green event! We could have lots of different stands, fundraising activities, make the event plastic free, use recycled materials, have a themed bake sale. . ."

"An upcycled art competition," Aaron jumps in.

"Yes!" I agree, and the pink in Aaron's cheeks gets darker. I look down and realize that in my excitement I've grasped his fingers in mine. I whip my hand away so fast it makes a whooshing sound through the air.

Aaron clears his throat. "Do you think we can get that organized in just over a week?"

"Easy," I say dismissively. "A piece of cake. Speaking of which, I think we need a biscuit top-up."

"Are you sure?" he asks. "I don't think your sister would be happy about that." He looks so serious that I get the giggles. Eventually Aaron joins in too, and I realize it's nice laughing with Aaron, and that it feels sort of normal (which is actually sort of weird).

We're interrupted by the sound of the front door opening. Mum's home. She opens the door to the living room and bustles in, pink-cheeked, her phone pressed between her ear and her shoulder as she wrestles to take her coat off.

"Not at all," she's saying, "I think it's a wonderful idea. The girls will be thrilled, and Dimitri too of course." She pauses and then chuckles. "Yes, you're probably right. We'll talk about it tomorrow. OK, see you soon, bye."

She chucks her phone to one side. "Hello, you two!" she says. "Aaron, what a nice surprise."

"We're collaborating on a Green Deal." I jump to my feet. "We're going to save the river! We're going to make the school eco-friendly!"

"How nice," Mum says, a mischievous twinkle in her eye. "It looks like you two are the dream team again!"

I feel my own cheeks flare pink at that. Honestly, parents. What a liability. I can't imagine Michelle Obama having to deal with this sort of nonsense.

"Who was that on the phone?" I ask, to distract her.

"It was Yia-yia," Mum says, as Dad appears carrying a big cup of coffee. "Oh, thank you, you wonderful man," she says, taking the cup from him and giving him a smacking great kiss.

How humiliating. I can't bring myself to look at Aaron.

"How was work?" Dad asks.

Mum makes a sound like the air being let out of a balloon. "Didn't get very far." She frowns. "I can't seem to track down anything more complete than the fragments I have and—"

"What did Yia-yia say?" I ask quickly. It's hard to stop Mum once she starts talking about something she cares about – I definitely inherited that from her.

Mum sips her coffee. "She's coming to visit next week!"

"Really?" I ask, pleased. "Is Papou coming too?"

Mum shakes her head. "He'll join us later. I think Yia-yia wants you to herself for a bit."

"And to do some shopping without him interfering," Dad laughs. He's probably right. Yia-yia is not really like the sort of grandma you might imagine. She's the most glamorous person I've ever met, sort of like Cruella de Vil but much less evil.

Aaron gets to his feet. "I'd better get home."

"Would you like to stay for dinner?" Dad asks.

"No, thank you," Aaron says. "Mum's expecting me. And I'm meeting up with Matt later."

I try to stop my face from making an expression like I've bitten into a sour lemon. Aaron might be bearable sometimes, but he's got truly horrible taste in friends.

"Have fun," I say as Aaron gathers his stuff together.

"Yeah." He flashes me a grin. "Let's pick this up tomorrow."

"Sure," I agree, walking with him back to the front hall.

"Your mum is right. We really do make a good team," Aaron says. Then he holds his fist out to me.

I stare at it blankly. Aaron chuckles and reaches out for my hand, folds my fingers into a fist, then bumps our hands together.

"Later, Kostas." He swings his bag on his shoulder and disappears out the door into the cold.

I stand for a moment, staring at the space where he was. There's a sudden tingly feeling shooting up and down my arm. *Probably just the chill from outside,* I tell myself, closing the door with a click.

CHAPTER *Six*

Highworth Grange School Council Meeting – 12 March

Minutes recorded by Angelika Lisowski

Meeting called to order at 3.30 p.m. by meeting chair Mr Jameson.

Members present:

Chair Mr Jameson (new physics teacher)
Aaron Davis (junior student president)
Matt Spader (junior student vice president)
Angelika Lisowski (junior student secretary)

Charlotte Hoskins (junior student treasurer)
Effie Kostas (activist, glitter glue enthusiast, true friend)

Reading of Agenda

- First of all, Miss Sardana sends her apologies. She is on leave for the next few weeks. Mr Jameson will fill in as chair for student council.
- Mr Jameson reads the agenda. Today we will discuss the school fete. Effie Kostas is here to talk about a school-wide recycling programme, which this completely impartial observer thinks sounds great.
- Mr Jameson agrees the agenda.

New Business

- Effie Kostas wants to use some of the council budget to initiate a GREEN NEW DEAL at Highworth Grange.
- Matt Spader makes a snorting noise. He suggests there are better things to spend the budget on. He has some ideas.

- Charlotte Hoskins interrupts to ask if anyone has seen her gloves.
- There is a brief pause as everyone looks for the gloves. Apparently these are the third pair Charlotte has lost. Her mum is going to kill her.
- Matt suggests that "Ellie" (I assume he means Effie) is a sore loser who can't just let the elected council get on with their jobs.
- Aaron says he thinks Effie's ideas are good and that Matt should give them a chance.
- Matt looks like he swallowed a bug.
- Effie thanks Aaron graciously and produces a ring binder to outline her scheme in more detail.
- Matt looks a bit sick.
- Effie outlines the new GREEN DEAL:
  Phase one: a recycling scheme and a local river clean-up. The date for the river clean-up will be the first Saturday of the Easter holidays.
  Phase two: the establishment of a vegetable garden, wormery and compost station.
- Charlotte Hoskins announces she has located one glove.

- Aaron explains the school fete will be a green event.
- Aaron and Effie grin at each other. Truly inspiring to see two former rivals are coming together to work on something so positive.
- Charlotte says the glove she has found is not hers.
- Matt says actually *he* had some ideas about the school fete. He thinks the money should go towards buying new kits for the football team. Something to do with changing them from red to blue. (Probably so they match his eyes.)
- Aaron says the football uniforms can wait until next term.
- Matt is glaring at Effie like she ate the last slice of chocolate cake.
- Aaron calls for a vote on the motion to approve the Green Deal and to move forward with phase one.
- The vote passes unanimously (although Matt looks sulky).
- Charlotte produces another glove from her pocket.

- That one isn't hers either.

Meeting adjourned at 4.00 p.m.

CHAPTER *Seven*

The next day I'm walking to school still buzzing from our successful student council meeting when I hear a voice calling my name. "Effie! Effie, wait up!"

I turn around, surprised to find Katie running towards me. Her long hair is swinging in a high ponytail, and a pair of fluffy grey earmuffs frame her face.

"Are you calling me?" I ask her.

"No, I was calling some other Effie," she giggles, confusing me further by tucking her hand through my arm. Her hand, I notice, is clad in a grey mitten that matches her earmuffs.

"Did you want something?" I ask, a bit more bluntly than I meant to.

Katie wrinkles up her nose a little. "I wanted to talk to you," she says sweetly. "I know we've had our differences, but don't you think we should try and get along? For Aaron's sake."

"What does Aaron have to do with anything?" I ask.

Katie shrugs. "Well, it looks like this Green Deal thing is going to happen . . . congrats on that, by the way."

"Thanks," I say, still puzzled.

"So you and Aaron will be spending loads of time together, and Aaron and I are, well, very good friends, so we should be too."

I stare at her for a second. Her face is hard to read. "OK," I say. "Friends."

Several emotions flicker across Katie's eyes: surprise, triumph, suspicion. "Good," she says.

"So," I say, "do you want to come over after school?"

"What?!" Katie says, looking startled. I bite back a laugh.

"That's what friends do, isn't it?" I ask innocently. "Angelika's coming over too, so we can all hang out together." I smile at her. I make it my best smile.

"What are you doing with your face?" She frowns.

"I'm trying to give you a sincere but not

overpowering smile."

"You're so weird," Katie says, but there is something like a laugh hiding at the back of her words. "I guess I can come over for a bit."

"Cool," I say. "I'll meet you by the gates at the end of the day then."

"Fine," she says, and swishes off ahead of me, calling out to one of her friends who's just turned on to the road.

Well, I think. *This is going to be interesting.*

I meet Angelika at our campaign office, where she is finessing the beautiful sign Kevin has made to raise awareness of the river clean-up. We've also set up a donations box. I tell her we have another guest this evening and she is definitely not impressed.

"Katie?!" she asks, as if I've just told her I've invited Darth Vader over for tea. "You asked Katie? Why would you do that?"

I shrug as we head out into the corridor, shutting the office door behind us. "She said she wanted us to be friends."

"And you believed her?" Angelika says.

"I don't know." I stop at my locker and quickly stuff my French textbook inside. "I hate all this stupid mean girls stuff. We should be sticking together. And I'm feeling generous thanks to my STUNNING VICTORY at student council last night."

The conversation is paused briefly as Angelika and I take part in an elaborate celebratory handshake that finishes with us dancing around in a circle.

"Plus," I continue once we're done, "I thought I could win Katie over with my charm and wit."

Angelika snorts.

"What?" I exclaim. "I can be VERY charming!"

"Of course," Angelika says quickly. "But you're forgetting, I've known Katie for a long time and she doesn't do anything without an ulterior motive."

I had forgotten that Katie and Angelika were best friends at primary school. Katie dropped Angelika like a hot potato when they got to secondary school. Angelika doesn't talk about it much, but I know it hurt her feelings. It makes it hard to warm to Katie – Angelika is objectively the best human in the world, and I can't even imagine not wanting to be her friend. Now I feel guilty that I invited Katie over at all.

Angelika must see something in my face because she smiles reassuringly. "I'll be fine," she says. "I've got your back."

"And I've got yours," I say firmly. "Plus, I *shall* win her over. With charm and Dad's revani."

Angelika grins. "Do you think if you sat all the world leaders down over your dad's revani we'd have world peace?"

"I guess we'll find out when I'm prime minister," I say as the bell rings.

When we first meet after school there's a definite chill between Katie and Angelika, but they manage to be polite and by the time we reach my house, things are even a little friendly.

Soon we're sitting at my kitchen table with huge slices of revani and gently steaming mugs of hot chocolate with whipped cream.

"This cake is, like, seriously amazing," Katie says, picking up crumbs with her fingers.

"It's my yia-yia's recipe," I say, taking a slurp of my hot chocolate. "She's coming to stay soon, and there will be SO MANY good treats."

"I am very excited." Angelika grins, a whipped cream moustache on her upper lip.

"She's Greek, right?" Katie asks.

I nod. "Yeah, my dad was born in Greece. They moved over here from Samos when he was little."

"That's cool," Katie says. "We went on holiday to Crete last year and it was awesome."

"Lucky you," I sigh. "We haven't been since I was about three. Lil wasn't even born then."

"Did someone say my name?" Lil's voice comes from the door. She's been over at a friend's, presumably running her tiny empire.

Katie splutters into her hot chocolate cup and I turn to see that Lil is wearing one of the costumes Dad made for her on his ancient sewing machine. I have to admit this one is a bit startling – she's dressed as Maui from *Moana*, complete with a tan-coloured bodysuit bursting with muscles made from pillow stuffing and black ink tattoos. She carries a cardboard hook in her hand.

"Nice costume, Lils," Angelika says admiringly, and Lil beams.

"It's a good one, isn't it?" she says. She looks at Katie. "What do you think?"

I watch Katie carefully. She's behaved well so far, but if she says anything mean to Lil then I will *have* to swear vengeance and find a way to destroy her and any chance of peace between us will be gone.

"I think it's amazing!" Katie exclaims, getting to her feet to have a closer look. "Maui, right?"

Lil grins and breaks into a few lines of "You're Welcome", and to my surprise, Katie joins in.

"You're a *Moana* fan?" Angelika asks Katie.

Katie flushes. "Aaron and I used to watch it with his little sister," she says.

"Enough times that you know all the words?" I ask with a raised eyebrow.

A reluctant smile tugs at Katie's mouth. "I might have watched it once or twice on my own since," she admits.

"You're a friend of Aaron's?" Lil asks, her face darkening. Her eyes flicker towards our empty plates. "Are you eating Dad's revani?" she says, dangerously quiet.

There's a pause.

"Have you got a copy of *Moana*?" Katie asks brightly, breaking the silence. "Because we could watch it now, if you wanted."

"And I'll get you a piece of cake," Angelika says swiftly.

Lil inclines her head like the queen. "That would be acceptable," she says, flopping on the sofa in a way that makes all her fake muscles bunch up around her ears.

By the time Mum gets home, Katie's wearing a grass skirt over her school uniform and we're all swaying around the living room singing "How Far I'll Go" at the top of our lungs.

"Thanks for having me over," Katie says later, as we're standing by the front door. "I actually had a good time."

"You don't need to sound so surprised," I reply. "It was nice. Let's do it again sometime."

"Don't get ahead of yourself, Effie Kostas," she says, putting on her earmuffs, but she's smiling a small, but real, smile.

If me and Katie can actually get along, then anything is possible, I think, shutting the door. Maybe one day me and Matt Spader will end up sharing cake and singing Disney songs.

"Don't get ahead of yourself, Effie Kostas," I say, and then I go back through to join Angelika and

Lil, who are discussing how to make a giant crab costume out of egg boxes.

CHAPTER *Eight*

CANDIDATES REUNITE IN SHOCK MOVE BY COUNCIL.

By Catriona McGiddens

Students were left all a-twitter over the weekend when news leaked that studly student council president Aaron Davis was seen spending time with his one-time **POLITICAL NEMESIS**, Effie Kostas, the girl with big hair and even bigger ideas. A secret source inside the administration revealed

EXCLUSIVELY to us that Aaron and Effie have joined forces to tackle Highworth Grange's eco credentials. (Our source also asks that if anyone finds a black glove with purple piping please can they turn it in to Lost Property.)

So, dear readers, is this the return of Team #EffRon? Let's not forget that only a few short months ago, RUMOURS WERE SWIRLING that these political rivals were more than just frenemies...

But another year-nine student had a different take. "Aaron **HAS** to work with Ellie – I mean, Effie – but he's not happy about it. She's just jealous. He's president and she's not and she needs to get over it. It's embarrassing."

Whatever the truth, it's **HARD TO DENY** the success of the winter dance organized by these two (hello, did you **SEE** that reindeer?!! #SantasSquadGoals). This reporter can't wait to see what they dream up.

As to the question of whether there's more than business between Effie and Aaron ... **ONLY TIME WILL TELL...**

The next day, I'm sitting in my campaign office waiting for Aaron. We arranged to meet up and talk about the school fete and I was looking forward to it, but that was before the stupid school paper printed a particularly stupid story. I'm feeling fairly furious, especially about the horrible quote that is so obviously from Matt. Ugh, that guy is the WORST.

I straighten the notebooks on my desk. Catriona, the editor of the paper, is almost as bad. Saying all that stuff about me and Aaron, when it's not even REMOTELY true. Honestly, journalistic standards in this school are the pits. Next thing you know she'll be wiretapping all our phones and going through people's bins.

There's a knock at the door. I take a deep breath, determined to be an unruffled professional.

"Come in!" I call, in my best "I'm-busy-leading-this-country-but-I-still-have-time-for-the-little-people" voice. I press my palms flat against the desk and rise graciously but with a kind of commanding dignity.

"Aaron," I say in businesslike tones as he walks through the door. "Please, take a seat." I gesture to the purple beanbag in front of the table.

"Er, thanks," Aaron says as he lowers himself with a not-so-graceful thud.

He smiles at me and I start to smile back before I remember the conversation I need to have.

"Thank you for coming," I say. "Now, first I wanted to clear something up. As you may know, there was an unfortunate report in the student paper today."

Aaron flushes, which makes him look surprisingly adorable.

Think calming thoughts, Effie, I tell myself. *The smell of freshly sharpened pencils, Lin-Manuel Miranda's goatee, a perfectly organized bookcase.* I exhale slowly through my nose. This meditation business is actually pretty effective.

"I hope you know I had nothing to do with that article," Aaron is saying, and I snap back to attention. "I would never tell a reporter such a pack of wild lies."

I sigh. "I just wish your friends felt the same."

"My friends?" Aaron looks puzzled. "What do they have to do with this?"

"Come on," I say. "We both know it was Matt Spader who said that stuff about me."

"Matt?" Aaron says, surprised. "No way."

"Um, yes way," I say. "He's the only one who calls me Ellie, remember?"

"Calm down, Nancy Drew," Aaron snaps. "Just because he got your name wrong once, doesn't mean it was Matt. He wouldn't do that. I should know. I'm his best friend."

"Which just goes to show what very bad taste you have," I snap right back. "I don't get why you can't see what a jerk he is."

"And I don't get why you're laying into him for no reason." Aaron tries to jump angrily to his feet, which is easier said than done when you're squished into a beanbag. I look briefly away as Aaron extracts himself, so as to allow him to keep his dignity. "You'd go mad if I said something like that about one of your friends," he says finally, his struggle with the beany monster complete.

I feel suddenly deflated. Aaron's right. If he ever said anything mean about my friends I'd defend them UNTO THE DEATH. I might not like Matt Spader, but I suppose I have to admire Aaron's loyalty.

"You're right," I say. "I'm sorry I said he was a jerk. I still think it was him," I can't help adding in a rush.

"We will have to agree to disagree on that," says Aaron stiffly. He sounds like a grown-up and I remember that I'd wanted to be presidential and unruffled. That hasn't worked out so well. I'm as ruffled as the crinkliest cut crisp.

"Let's just focus on the fete, shall we," I say.

"We need to present our ideas to the council in a couple of days."

"Fine," Aaron says, folding himself carefully back into the beanbag and pulling his backpack towards him. "There's lots to do. I've made a list. . ."

The rest of our meeting goes OK. We discuss the different stands and who we could approach to run them, and we make more plans for our "upcycling" table where people can make art out of things that would otherwise be destined for the bin.

We're also going to do a bake sale to raise money for our river clean-up. (There isn't much in our donation box yet.) I'm going to run this with my friends so we can also sign people up for the actual clean-up at the same time. (It's much easier to convince people to do things when you're holding out a cupcake.)

We finish up so that Aaron can go to football practice, and this time he doesn't offer me a fist bump. Not that I wanted one.

I'm sitting at my desk, staring thoughtfully into the middle distance, when the door swings open. For a second I think it might be Aaron again, but it's not. It's Matt Spader.

"Matthew," I spit out icily.

"Eleanor." Matt grins at me – the smug grin of entitlement.

"It's Euphemia," I grind out. "Effie for short. AS I THINK YOU KNOW."

Matt shrugs and runs his eyes dismissively around the room. "I guess Aaron's already gone then."

"Unless he's turned into a purple beanbag," I say sweetly.

"Whatever." Matt goes to leave.

"I know it was you," I hiss. "That stupid quote in the paper. You might have Aaron fooled, but I know what you're really like."

"I don't know what you're talking about." Matt's smile is like a Halloween mask. "And Aaron is *my* friend, not yours. I think you'd better remember that."

With that he sweeps out of the room, leaving me staring after him, a hollow feeling in my chest.

When I walk out of the school gates a few minutes later, I see that it's started to snow, just a little bit. Usually, that would fill me with glee (snowmen! Snowball fights! Drinking hot chocolate!) but now I just feel miserable. I can still see Matt's horrible smile in my head. It sucks that Aaron and I aren't getting on – we had just started being friends. Plus, it's snowing in the middle of March when it should be all spring and lambs and new flowers, and the fact that the weather is all messed up only reminds me of the reasons behind the Green Deal in the first place.

I straighten my shoulders. I need to make sure we succeed. I can't let a stupid boy get in my way.

Something emerges on the path, a tall figure covered in fur, fat snowflakes falling around it. *A yeti*, I think wildly. I stop in my tracks, wondering exactly what the right etiquette is when one encounters a yeti on one's walk home. The yeti is tall and thin and as it moves a clip-clip-clipping noise echoes on the pavement. I rub my eyes and then I hear an impatient voice call out.

"Don't I get a hug, *Effitsa*? Or must I freeze to death first?"

"Yia-yia?" I say. "Is that you?"

"Who else?" the yeti says, majestically.

I run towards her and am immediately wrapped in a warm hug. Very warm – Yia-yia is wearing an enormous fur coat and a matching fur hat. Her green eyes twinkle in her perfectly made-up face and her mouth is a slash of crimson lipstick. The clip, clip, clip sounds were from her high heels striking the pavement.

"I like your coat," I say. "Except I'm obviously VERY anti-fur."

"Oh, Effitsa," Yia-yia says, putting her arm around my shoulders and turning for home. "Of course it isn't real. I do not need to murder anything to look fantastic."

I smile. Yia-yia is here and everything feels brighter. This day is looking up.

CHAPTER *Nine*

"It's SNOWWWWWINGGGGGGG," Lil yells when she meets us on the garden path. Her cheeks are pink and she's wrapped up in a purple sparkly snowsuit. "LET'S BUILD A SNOWMAN, SEE IF HE COMES TO LIFE AND THEN WE CAN BEFRIEND HIM AND HE WILL BE OUR SIDEKICK ON A QUEST AND I THINK WE SHOULD CALL HIM CARROT-NOSE OR MR FREEZE," she continues breathlessly.

I don't want to be the person to point out that there's not even a centimetre of snow on the ground yet, so instead I say, "Yia-yia's here!"

"I know *that*," Lil says witheringly. "She's been here for ages."

"Almost an hour," Yia-yia agrees.

"Exactly," Lil says. "Keep up, Effie." She snaps her fingers. "This is a twenty-four-hour news cycle, and the latest headline is that IT. IS. SNOWING."

"Lil, come inside!" Dad calls from the doorway. "There's not enough snow for a snowman yet, and Yia-yia wants a cup of tea."

"The first thing I'm going to get my magical snowman to do is put a curse on silly grown-ups who don't understand the first thing about snow," my sister mutters darkly.

"Come on," I say encouragingly. "Why don't we go in and you can show Yia-yia your interpretive dance to 'Let It Go'."

"Mmm." Lil tips her head thoughtfully. "All right. Perhaps the dance will act as a sort of snow summoning."

"Perhaps," I agree.

"Also, I need a biscuit," Yia-yia says. "I brought some with me. Now let's go inside before my toes drop off. Dimitri, I hope you have some good tea and not the rubbish you had last time I was here. I don't care if it is good for you, liquorice tea is a crime against tea drinkers."

"As I said at the time, Mum, you didn't have to *have* the liquorice tea, I was just letting you know that we had all sorts," Dad says wearily, making his way through to the living room as we all start wrestling with our layers of clothing. "Peppermint, lemon and ginger, summer berry..."

"Berry." Yia-yia shudders, shrugging out of her coat, which Lil immediately tries on. "Imagine the Queen hearing that."

Yia-yia loves the Queen and often talks about her as if she were her close personal friend. When Yia-yia and Papou moved to England from Greece, Yia-yia threw herself into being British with such enthusiasm that she practically became a member of the royal family.

"Well, in the unlikely event that the Queen pops round, I'll be sure to get the Tetley out." Dad grins.

"Her Majesty likes Earl Grey, Dimitri, as do I." She sinks into the sofa. "With the tiniest splash of milk."

"Coming right up, Your Highness." Dad bows elaborately.

"Yia-yia, this coat makes me feel MIGHTY," Lil says, sweeping in, the far-too-long fur trailing behind her.

"As all the best clothes should," Yia-yia says serenely. "Now, Effitsa, you looked sad when you were walking home from school. Why?"

"Did you have another fight with Aaron?" Lil asks.

"Aaron?" Yia-yia raises a perfectly arched eyebrow, looking suddenly exactly like Lil.

"Sort of," I sigh. "It was about his friend, Matt Spader. He's been saying things about me to the school paper." I frown. "Aaron was angry I accused his friend."

"Do you know for sure it was him?" asks Yia-yia.

"I think it was. But I don't have any proof."

"Well, it seems to me that you should get some, in that case." Yia-yia accepts a dainty cup and saucer that only comes out when she visits. She takes a sip. "Always so much more satisfying to know one is angry with the right person."

"Maybe you're right," I say thoughtfully.

"Or I could handle it," Lil says. "I know people who can take care of things."

"All right, Al Capone," Dad says. "That's quite enough of that. Why don't you give me a hand in the kitchen." When she doesn't move, he says temptingly, "Yia-yia brought kourabiedes."

"KOURABIEDES?!" Lil yelps, and then she's off, faster than a speeding bullet.

"Kourabiedes and snow," she sighs minutes later when we're all nibbling on delicious almondy biscuits. "Best. Day. Ever."

*

Much to Lil's disgust, the snow didn't really amount to anything, and the next day is just cold and slightly wet again. Even an optimist like myself knows it's hard to find much magic in damp grey days. I pull my Gryffindor scarf more tightly around my neck as I trudge to school. Maybe I should get some of those fluffy earmuffs like Katie has.

I should also take Yia-yia's advice. I can't take down Matt without proof. Perhaps if I could reveal him as the terrible person he is, then Aaron would stop taking his side.

"Hey! Effie!" a voice calls as I reach the school gates, and I see Ruby walking towards me, with Kevin in her wake.

"Hi, guys." I smile. "What's going on?"

"Didn't you hear the news?" Kevin asks breathlessly.

I look at them blankly. "What news?"

"It's all over the school!" he squeaks.

"But I've just arrived at school," I point out reasonably, "and you must have done too."

"You know it doesn't take us long to sniff out the gossip," Ruby says, flashing me a grin.

"Well, what is it?" I ask. "Don't tell me a bird got into the science block again."

"Nothing as trivial as that," says Kevin (who singlehandedly started the #SaveFeathers campaign).

"It's Aaron." Ruby pauses dramatically. "There's been a MURDER!"

My mouth drops open. "What?" I croak.

"Aaron's football career," Ruby exclaims. "It's been murdered!"

"Oh my god, Ruby!" I say as my pulse returns to a more normal pace. "You almost gave me a heart attack."

"That's rich, coming from you." Ruby folds her arms across her chest. "You're one of the most dramatic people I know."

"WHEN have I EVER been dramatic?" I cry, throwing my hands in the air.

I pause. "Point taken. So, what's happened to Aaron's football career then?"

"He broke his leg," Kevin explains. "At practice yesterday. He must have slipped in the snow. They had to call an ambulance and everything."

"Oh." I feel a pang of sympathy for Aaron. He loves football. "That's horrible." I also feel guilty. I was hoping I'd see him today to make up.

Ruby grimaces. "He's going to be off school for weeks."

"Lucky him," sighs Kevin.

"That's a long time," I say.

"Aaron's dad isn't taking any chances." Ruby shrugs. "He's convinced Aaron is the next David Beckham."

"I heard his dad's getting him some crazy-expensive physiotherapist to start working with him as soon as possible," Kevin adds. "And a tutor so he doesn't fall behind at school.

"Wow." Suddenly I realize something. "What about the fete?" I exclaim. "It's next week!"

"Not sure," says Ruby. "It's usually the student council president who organizes it."

"And if Aaron's not here then according to the rules, there's only one person who can replace him." I stop as the terrible realization hits me. Ruby and Kevin are wearing horror-stricken expressions that must match my own.

With one voice we utter the dreaded words:

"Matt Spader!"

CHAPTER *Ten*

The Highworth Grange Chronicle   Issue No. 215   21 March

PRESIDENT IN LEG SMASH SHOCKER!

By Catriona McGiddens

The school was left **REELING** today as student council president, star footballer and all-around Mr Popular, Aaron Davis, has been injured in a **SHOCK ACCIDENT** that may have ended his football career for good.

While practising last night, Aaron fell and **SHATTERED** his leg into a hundred pieces (a rough estimate; this reporter was unable to get Aaron's doctor on the phone despite frequent attempts). Exact details of the event are hazy. "Someone ran into Aaron, and the snow had just started so the ground was more slippy," one witness says. "He was so brave and his face went all pale like one of those Twilight vampires."

AND THIS PAPER CAN EXCLUSIVELY REVEAL THAT THIS SENSELESS TRAGEDY COULD HAVE BEEN AVOIDED.

Our unnamed source said: "This is yet more evidence that we need to change our football uniforms without delay. If Aaron had been wearing a pale blue uniform, then the light would have reflected better and he wouldn't have been knocked over. We've been calling for new uniforms for months now. It's just sad that Aaron had to pay the price."

Sad news indeed and surely a **RALLYING CRY** for fundraising efforts from the rest of the school.

It's not just the football team that will suffer from the absence of Aaron's left foot. The junior school council now finds itself without its leader, although vice president Matt Spader has rushed to reassure students that he will see the school through these **DIFFICULT TIMES**.

"If Highworth Grange was a boat then I would be its captain, sailing it through stormy waters," he said. "There is no need for students to worry. This administration has everything under control."

Reassuring words in uncertain times. Truly, the stuff of great leadership. **More on this story as it happens...**

CHAPTER *Eleven*

Highworth Grange School Council Meeting – 21 March

Minutes recorded by Angelika Lisowski

Meeting called to order at 3.30 p.m. by meeting chair Mr Jameson.

Members present:

Chair Mr Jameson
Matt Spader (**ACTING** junior student president, but **ACTUALLY** junior student vice president)
Angelika Lisowski (junior student secretary)

Charlotte Hoskins (junior student treasurer)
Effie Kostas (advocate, Disney fan)

Reading of Agenda

- Mr Jameson reads the agenda. Mr Jameson says that as Aaron is off school with a broken leg, Matt Spader will be acting president.
- Update on school fete. Effie takes out a binder.
- Update interrupted: Charlotte Hoskins asks if anyone has seen her pen? It is purple.
- There is a brief pause as we look for the pen. It is found by Effie.
- Effie explains that she and Aaron have been working on the fete and that they have some exciting ideas.
- Matt interrupts in a sort of super-smooth voice to say that it's usually the president who is in charge of organizing the fete.
- Charlotte Hoskins asks if anyone has seen her rubber. It is shaped like a unicorn but most of the horn has been rubbed off.
- There is a brief pause while we look for the rubber. We do not find it.
- Mr Jameson says we should get back on track.

- Effie reminds Matt he is the **ACTING** president.
- Matt reminds Effie that the rules are the rules and then he asks Mr Jameson if he agrees.
- Mr Jameson clears his throat and agrees nervously that rules are usually rules, yes.
- Matt says thank you to Mr Jameson and gives him a big smile. He says Mr Jameson is doing a great job as council chairman.
- Effie points out that it's chair**PERSON**, and that Miss Sardana usually does a great job, and that she's only on leave for a couple more weeks . . . just like Aaron, the **RIGHTFUL PRESIDENT.**
- Matt says that he has lots of ideas for the fete and he doesn't need Effie's help any further, but thanks her for what she's done so far.
- Angelika Lisowski – who for clarity is also writing these minutes – agrees that it is ridiculous to throw out all of Effie and Aaron's hard work.
- Mr Jameson mumbles something about Effie and Matt maybe working together.
- Effie and Matt both shout **NO**.
- Charlotte Hoskins has found her rubber. It

was in her pencil case the whole time.

- Matt says he also has a piece of new business. He wants to introduce a new system of prefects, to help keep the school running smoothly, in the "turmoil" surrounding Aaron's absence.
- Matt says that the prefect system is in place at other schools – that prefects just make sure people are obeying rules and act as role models for younger students. It teaches leadership and responsibility and looks really good when people apply for college to have it on their application.
- Mr Jameson says that's very thoughtful and he'll raise it with the head. And that now he needs to go and move his car. He says he's sure Matt will do a fine job on the fete and calls the meeting to an end.
- Mr Jameson scurries out as fast as possible.
- Matt Spader is grinning like an evil cartoon shark.

Meeting adjourned at 4.00 p.m.

CHAPTER *Twelve*

"I can't believe it!" I say to Angelika the next morning. It's about the fiftieth time I've said it since the meeting last night. "Just like that, all our hard work is out the window. How could Matt do that?"

Angelika is frowning fiercely, her blonde ponytail bobbing angrily as she walks with me towards our maths lesson. "Matt Spader won't get away with this," she says. "We have to do something. Otherwise the fete is going to be all about raising money for blue football uniforms instead of anything worthwhile."

"And Mr Jameson wasn't much help," I add. "You'd think he'd never been in a high-stakes political situation before. Honestly, sometimes grown-ups can be useless."

"He was worse than useless!" Angelika exclaims. "He's so obviously on Matt's side. Joking around like they were best friends. If Miss Sardana had been there it would have been different."

"Curse that research fellowship," I bellow.

"Effie!" Angelika looks shocked.

I take a deep, shuddering breath. "You're right, you're right, I take it back. You know I'm very supportive of the arts. I'm just frustrated!"

I clutch my beautiful binder in my arms as we sit down at our desk. It's full of the work Aaron and I have done. I feel sick thinking about Matt Spader's smug face.

"Maybe you should go and talk to Aaron," Angelika whispers as our maths teacher, Mr Blake, tells us which problems to start on. "If you can get past his dad, that is."

The last time I saw Aaron, he was busy defending Matt. There's no way he's going to be on my side now.

"I don't think that will help," I hiss back. "Aaron will never side with me over him."

"I hope you two are talking about maths, girls," says Mr Blake, appearing suddenly at my shoulder.

I feel a rush of heat to my cheeks. Now I'm getting in trouble with teachers as well. "Oh, we were, sir," I say quickly. "Numbers! Love them, can't get enough of them ... um, multiplying and dividing ... equations and triangles and the like ... and pi!" I exclaim suddenly. "Who doesn't like pi?"

"That's the spirit, Effie," says Mr Blake. "I like to hear this kind of enthusiasm in the morning." He pushes his glasses up on his nose. "Had no idea you were a fellow enthusiast. How many digits of pi can you remember?"

"Um," I say weakly, "three?"

"Three?" Mr Blake frowns.

"Thousand," I say quickly, physically unable to disappoint a teacher.

"Goodness!" Mr Blake's eyes widen. "That *is* impressive. You'll have to do a demonstration for the class!"

"Actually, sir." Angelika leaps in like a selfless bodyguard diving right between me and a speeding bullet. "I wondered if I could ask you a question about the homework? I was bit confused by question three."

"Oh yes," Mr Blake says eagerly. "That *was* a bit tricky. Class!" He calls everyone to attention. "Can we all open our textbooks to page forty-seven and tackle the homework questions together."

"Thank you," I whisper to Angelika. "You're a lifesaver."

Angelika grins. "Don't thank me yet," she says. "At some point he's going to remember to ask you about it again."

"You're right," I say glumly, "I suppose I'm going to have to try and memorize three thousand numbers then."

The rest of the maths class passes without incident, and I pack up my backpack rather speedily at the end, while carefully avoiding eye contact with Mr Blake. Angelika stays behind, asking him another question, just to ensure my escape. Truly, she is the greatest.

I bustle out of the classroom at speed, and right into the smug golden face of Matt Spader.

"You!" I hiss, like we're at the panto and the villain has just appeared onstage.

Matt looks down at me like he barely recognises me. "Ellie. Hello."

"It's Effie. And don't you *hello* me," I snap. "What was that stunt at the council meeting yesterday? I can't believe you're just going to chuck out all the work that me and Aaron did."

"Hey, Effie," I hear a voice say, and I see that Katie has appeared at Matt's shoulder.

"Hi, Katie," I say, not taking my eyes off Matt.

Matt's eyes flicker to Katie and then back to me, as though surprised that Katie is even acknowledging my existence. His nose wrinkles, like I'm a puzzle he can't understand.

"I'm sorry that we couldn't go ahead with your ideas, Effie," he says, getting my name right for the first time ever. "I'm doing what I think is best during this difficult time."

I take a deep breath. Being a politician means having to work with people you don't always agree with. I can play the game. "Of course you do," I say in my most soothing voice. "Surely we can reach a compromise. A split of the budget, perhaps?"

Matt shakes his head. "I'm afraid not," he says. "Confidentially, we've agreed to use the budget to hire a paintball service. And they need a lot of room so we haven't got space for the stands you wanted." He pats my arm. "It's a real shame, Effie. Next time we can definitely do your green thing."

"Paintball?!" I say. "Why are we having paintball?"

Matt smiles at me. "A survey of students showed they were very keen on paintball, Effie."

"I didn't get asked," I say.

"It was a sample survey," he says. "We are going to use your idea for the bake sale though, and you can remain in charge of that," he adds generously. "We'll use any funds raised for the extracurricular activity groups, real community service stuff. That's down to you."

My voice is tight as I reply. "By 'community service' and 'extracurricular activity groups' you wouldn't by any chance mean the boys' football team and the new uniforms, would you? Because that money was supposed to be going towards the river clean-up."

"A high-achieving sports group like the football team is ONE of the deserving groups we've selected," Matt says, smiling even harder. "After all, the boys' team made it to the semi-finals last year. We're ambassadors for the school. Students want to fundraise for things which affect them. What has a river clean-up got to do with us?"

"It's got everything to do with us!" I say hotly. "We should *all* be protecting the environment. Some of that rubbish might have come from this school! How can you possibly think football uniforms are more important than CLEAN WATER?"

Matt shrugs. He is still smiling his frozen grin. He's outsmarted me, I realize. The idea makes me want to throw up.

"Do the funds apply to the girls' team too?" Katie asks, breaking the silence. I'd forgotten she was there.

"Sorry," Matt says, turning his smile on her. "What was that?"

"I was just wondering if the girls' football team is getting some of the funds?" she says. She tosses her head slightly so that her ponytail ripples down her back. "If it's important that that the money stays in the school."

Matt's smile slips briefly. "Well, as you know, the girls' football team is relatively new," he continues smoothly. "They don't have the same requirements as the more established team. As soon as they start getting the big matches, then that will be another story," he adds encouragingly. "It's complicated, this sponsorship business. Lots of moving parts, as I'm finding out." He grins ruefully. "But we'll get there. The girls' football team is my top priority."

Katie narrows her eyes. But all she says is, "I understand."

I feel a pang of disappointment. For a moment there, I thought she might stand up against Matt.

"You seem to have misunderstood what the school council is there for," I say to Matt, still trying to keep my temper. "It's not just to help you get whatever you want. You're supposed to be working for the students."

"I am a student," Matt says. "And I think I know what students want." He takes a step closer. "The bottom line, Effie, is that I'm on student council, you're not. Get over it."

CHAPTER *Thirteen*

"Get over it?" Iris repeats later. "That's what he told you to do?"

I nod and play with the piece of cake in front of me. I headed straight over to Iris's when school finished, still feeling humiliated and helpless after my run-in with Matt. Even a giant wodge of coffee cake and all of Lennon the parrot's best insults are failing to lift my spirits.

Iris fixes me with a firm stare, and Lennon, perched on her shoulder, tips his head and does the same.

"It sounds to me like you've got him rattled," Iris says finally.

"He didn't seem rattled," I sigh.

There's a silence that stretches between us for a moment. Iris breaks it finally. "Effie," she says. "If you're going to be an activist then I'm afraid you're going to come up against a lot of Matt Spaders. People who want to belittle you and the cause you're fighting for. People who are afraid of change, or who have their own reasons for wanting things to stay the way they are." She reaches out and squeezes my hand, just for a second. "Do you believe what you're fighting for is right?"

"Yes," I say quickly. "I think raising money for the river clean-up is important. I think it's exactly the sort of thing the school SHOULD get involved in as part of the community. We shouldn't only be interested in what's going on inside the school gates . . . that's so narrow-minded and selfish. And damage to the environment affects all of us anyway!"

"Well then." Iris is brisk. "You've just got to keep fighting for it, haven't you? Where would we be if the suffragists just gave up when an obnoxious boy told them he didn't like what they were doing?"

"STUPID PEANUT," Lennon squawks.

"Matt IS a stupid peanut," I agree, thinking over what Iris has said. Suddenly I find maybe I can manage a piece of cake after all, and I take a big squishy bite.

Iris and I talk some more about the problems of being a trailblazer, until we are interrupted by the sound of the doorbell.

"Will you get that, Effie?" Iris asks. "Saves me struggling up. Probably the delivery person with my hair dye. Can't let it fade, can we?" She ruffles her pink hair, which is still almost as bright as the hot pink walls of her kitchen.

I leap up and go back through the house to open the door. Standing on the doorstep is no delivery man, but Yia-yia.

"Yia-yia!" I exclaim. "What are you doing here?"

"Your father told me you were here. I thought I should come and introduce myself to this neighbour you are all so fond of."

"Who is it, Effie?" Iris calls from the kitchen.

I lead Yia-yia through to the kitchen.

"This is my yia-yia," I say. "Yia-yia, this is Iris."

I feel a moment of unease as I watch Iris and Yia-yia sizing each other up. They are the two most formidable women I know, and they're very different. Iris, with her hot pink hair, her huge tasselly orange earrings and her neon-yellow tunic looks like she's from a different planet to Yia-yia, with her polished red nails, matching lipstick, chic cream silk blouse and wide black trousers. She has a huge pair of sunglasses balanced on top of her head, even though it's not actually sunny and she's only walked round from next door.

"I love your lipstick," Iris says finally.

"Those earrings are wonderful," Yia-yia says.

"Why don't join us for some cake?" says Iris.

"Thank you." Yia-yia slides into a seat.

"Your granddaughters are special girls," Iris says, a little grudgingly, casting me a look that tells me I shouldn't get ideas about how much she likes us or anything.

"They are *very* special girls," Yia-yia corrects her, majestically.

Iris sniffs and starts pouring out another cup of tea. Lennon hops across the table and with a flutter of his wings, he comes to perch on Yia-yia's shoulder. I've never seen him do that with anyone but Iris before.

"YOU TROUBLESOME BADGER!" Lennon squawks affectionately.

"Thank you, dear," Yia-yia replies, completely composed. "Iris, you must give me the recipe for this coffee cake. It is very good."

"Thank you," says Iris, inclining her head. "Your revani is excellent."

The two women eye each other beadily for a moment. And then they both grin, big grins. I let out a sigh of relief. At least one thing has gone right today.

CHAPTER *Fourteen*

The next day I arrive at school. I've decided to try and take Iris's advice. After all, if I want to become prime minister and sort the world out and ultimately become an inspiration to millions of young women, and start my own foundation where I rid the world of plastic, then I'm going to have to toughen up.

I join my friends in the queue for assembly. They're all chatting about baking ideas.

"We should make recycling-themed biscuits in the shape of the earth and recycling bins," Angelika says.

"What does a recycling-bin-shaped biscuit look like?" Jess asks.

"Kevin will work it out." I wave my hand airily.

"Um, sure." Kevin sounds less certain.

"AND," I say, "we can still have a sign-up sheet for volunteers. Matt can take away the fundraising bit, but we can still use it to do a lot of good."

The others chime in agreement as we file into the school hall and sit in neat rows.

"Right, everyone," Ms Shaarawi, the head teacher, says, clapping her hands together. "I have a couple of announcements to make. The first is that as you all probably already know, following Aaron Davies's football injury, Matt Spader has kindly agreed to step in as acting student council president." There's a scattered round of applause and Matt bounces up on to the stage, smiling and waving.

"Booooo," I hear Ruby hiss under her breath.

"Now, Matt has an exciting announcement that I'm going to let him talk to you about himself."

Matt grins winningly. "Thank you, miss," he says. "I am really excited today to talk about a brilliant new scheme that Aaron and I have been discussing for a while." He looks out over the audience. "I know Aaron is gutted not to be here himself to tell you all about it, and we all hope he has a speedy recovery."

"Whoop!" comes a cry from the audience.

Matt nods in acknowledgement. "Our idea is to introduce a prefect system to the school. Prefects will help to keep our hallways safe, they'll model excellent behaviour and act as representatives for the school. They'll report to student council, so they'll be another point of contact for students who have issues they want the council to address. Being a prefect will look amazing on your school record, and we encourage anyone who's interested to sign up on the sheet outside after assembly. We want students to feel seen and heard by this administration, and to reassure you all that even with Aaron gone . . . for who knows *how* long . . . everything will continue to run smoothly." He winks. "I have got you covered. Mr Jameson and I will look over the sign-up sheet and make a shortlist of candidates this afternoon based on people's school records. Then there will be a random selection to keep things fair. We'll notify you by the end of the day if you are successful."

He looks over to Ms Shaarawi, who smiles and nods encouragingly.

"I'll let miss get back to the assembly now. Thank you all for listening."

As Ms Shaarawi starts reading out various notices, I let my mind drift to consider all this new information. A prefect programme could be really good for this school – in fact, it's one of the ideas that

I myself dropped in Aaron's suggestion box. But if Matt's overseeing it then there must be some sinister agenda, mustn't there?

At the end of assembly my friends and I join the line to write our names on the list.

"This school would be lucky to have us," Ruby says.

By the end of the day it seems that the school is not so lucky after all.

We huddle in front of the list on the noticeboard.

"Andrew Gibbs, Dave Fletcher, Katie Thomas, Jordan James, Cam Singh." Angelika reads the names aloud in tones of dread.

"Is it just me. . ." Jess says.

"Or is that just a list of Matt's friends?" I finish. "Yes, it is. And you know what that means. . ." They all look at me wide-eyed. "Matt must have tampered with the results."

CHAPTER *Fifteen*

Things go from bad to worse the next afternoon.

It's lunchtime and I'm standing in the queue with Zo, my blue plastic tray in my hands. The others are already here, they've bagged us a table, and Zo and I wave over at them.

I pause in front of the drinks fridge. "Look at all that bottled water, Zo," I sigh. "Why can't people just use the water fountains and bring reusable bottles?"

"Because the water fountains never work," Zo says.

I groan. "Another thing to add to the list. Honestly, this school is in desperate need of—" My words are interrupted abruptly by the jostle of an elbow. Someone shoves Zo to one side, and she freezes up like a rabbit in the headlights. No one likes being shoved around but it's especially upsetting for Zo.

"OI!" I say, putting myself between Zo and the shover. "What are you doing? There's a queue, you know."

The boy turns around and I groan. It's one of Matt's pals, Dave Fletcher. My eyes drop to the lapel of his blazer, where a shining gold PREFECT badge gleams tauntingly out at me. I absolutely love a good badge, but this one makes me feel ill.

"I know there's a queue," Dave says. "But I've got this."

In his hand is a little laminated card with the words LUNCH PASS stamped across it. Exactly like the one Aaron Davis flashed at me the first time we met. It means that the student president can go to the front of the lunch queue.

I fold my arms across my chest. I can feel Zo hovering anxiously at my shoulder.

"Why do *you* have a lunch pass?" I ask dangerously. "You're not student president."

Dave simply turns his back to me as though I haven't spoken and scoops up a bottle of water.

"EXCUSE ME," I say. "You didn't answer my question. I want to know why you have a lunch pass."

"I'm a prefect," he replies, pointing to the shiny

badge. "See?"

"Yes, I can see your badge," I grind out. "The one you did NOTHING to earn. I still don't understand why you have a lunch pass."

Dave's forehead crinkles in confusion. "Dunno." He shrugs. "All the prefects do."

"Brilliant," I mutter under my breath. Just another example of these stupid boys abusing their privilege.

Dave is staring at me now. "You're that girl," he says slowly. "The one who Matt doesn't like. The bossy one."

"The word 'bossy' is sexist nonsense," I snap. "No one ever calls a boy bossy. When boys are bossy they're called leaders. When girls try to take charge then people call them bossy. It's stupid and it's lazy."

He points to my stomach. "Your shirt's untucked," he says.

I look down and the corner of my shirt has come loose. "Right," I say slowly. "What's it to you?"

"That's against the rules." He looks pleased with himself. "I'm giving you a demerit."

Now it's my turn to stare. "You're ... what?"

Dave pulls a notebook and pencil out of his pocket. "It's Ellie, right?"

"Effie," I correct him automatically.

"Weird name," he grunts, carefully writing my name in his book.

"I – I," I stutter. "What do you mean you're giving me a demerit?"

"That's my job," he says. "I make sure people follow the rules."

"But it wasn't on purpose," I say. I gesture to his shirt. "*Your* shirt is untucked too."

Dave shrugs again. "Whatever." He grabs his sandwich and walks away, leaving me standing, frozen, behind him.

"He . . . gave me . . . a demerit," I say slowly. "I've never had a demerit before."

"Let's go and sit with the others." Zo tugs gently at my arm. We grab our lunches and make our way over.

Zo gives them all a brief outline of what happened while I sit there in silence.

"They can give out demerits?" Angelika's eyes widen. "Well, that's new information."

"Don't worry about it, Effie," Ruby says. "Demerits aren't that big a deal."

"But I've never had one before!" I burst out. "And I hadn't noticed my shirt was untucked. It wasn't even fully untucked. I could have just fixed it. Even teachers let you have a chance to tuck your shirt in before they give you a demerit."

"Effie," Zo says. "I don't think it was really about your shirt."

"What do you mean?" I ask, puzzled.

"He didn't give you the demerit until he realized who you were. He said you were the girl Matt doesn't like."

I let her words sink in. "You mean . . . you mean. . ."

Angelika's eyes spark angrily. "Matt's using the prefects against you."

"No!" Jess looks shocked.

"He can't do that!" Kevin exclaims.

I stare miserably down at my cheese sandwich. "I think maybe he can."

A voice interrupts us then. "Effie Kostas?" It's a small blonde girl from year seven. "Ms Shaarawi wants to see you in her office." Silence falls. The others turn to me with concern all over their faces.

Summoned to the head teacher's office.

This day just keeps getting worse.

CHAPTER *Sixteen*

I arrive at Ms Shaarawi's office feeling very nervous. I knock tentatively on the door.

"Come in," a voice calls.

I push the door open to find two people inside. One of them is Ms Shaarawi. The other is a bit of a surprise.

"Yia-yia?"

Yia-yia is wearing her enormous fur coat, but she has swapped the furry hat for a small black one that has a little net veil over her face. It looks very dramatic with the red lipstick.

"Oh, Effie," she cries dramatically. "I have bad news about Great-Uncle Nestor!"

"Great-Uncle Nestor?" I repeat blankly. I've never heard of a Great-Uncle Nestor.

"He is VERRRY ill." Yia-yia flops dejectedly into a nearby chair, and Ms Shaarawi pats her hand.

"Oh dear," I murmur, trying to work out what is going on. With Yia-yia, there is always something going on.

"You poor thing," Yia-yia sighs. "You obviously cannot take it in. You are overwhelmed."

"Overwhelmed," I repeat.

Yia-yia gives me a hard stare. "Yes," she says, rising to her feet. "Overwhelmed. We must go to him now. Thank you, Ms Shaarawi, it was a pleasure meeting you, even under such sad circumstances."

"Of course," says Ms Shaarawi. She looks a bit dazed, which is often the effect that Yia-yia has on people.

"Come, Euphemia," Yia-yia commands, sweeping me from the room.

We're in the car park by the time I get my wits together enough to ask what is going on.

"*Who*," I ask, "is Great-Uncle Nestor?"

Yia-yia cackles. "Poor old Nestor, he is on his deathbed. Thank goodness he is made up."

I stare at her, even more confused. "You made him up?"

"Of course!" Yia-yia exclaims, pressing the button

on the car key with a cheery *bip-bip*. "I'm kidnapping you." She opens the car door.

I climb in and see that Lil is strapped into the back seat, wearing enormous sunglasses and slurping on a milkshake.

"Hi, Effie," she says. "Did you hear about Great-Uncle Festor?"

"Great-Uncle *Nestor*," Yia-yia corrects her, casting off the little black hat and putting on a pair of enormous tortoiseshell sunglasses. "One must always keep one's story straight, Lilika."

"Got it." Lil nods coolly.

"Oh my gosh," I gasp as the pieces fall into place. "You're sneaking me out of school? Couldn't you go to prison or something? Couldn't we ALL go to prison??"

"Calm down, Effie," Yia-yia says soothingly, clipping in her seat belt. "If it makes you feel better, your mum and dad gave me a note to get you out of school for this afternoon. But I always think a little drama adds to the experience."

"Okayyyy," I say, cautiously doing up my seat belt. "That's a bit better, I suppose." There's a strawberry milkshake in the drinks holder waiting for me. Lil hands me my own pair of sunglasses. I put them on and instantly feel like a bit of Yia-yia's glamour has rubbed off on me.

"This is exactly your problem," Yia-yia says, starting the car. "You need to relax the rules a little sometimes."

"I happen to like rules," I say, thinking about Matt and his abuse of the system. "They help things make sense."

Yia-yia slides her glasses down her nose and darts a look at me over the top of them. "Something is wrong?"

"I – I. . ." I start, but then it's like all of the drama of the last hour catches up with me, and even though I am thirteen and a future world leader, I burst into noisy tears.

Yia-yia pulls the car swiftly over to the side of the road and gathers me into her arms, my face buried in her soft furry coat.

"Now," she says gently, once my tears calm down. "What is going on?"

I tell her and Lil what happened. For a moment the car is silent.

"I will go and talk to Ms Shaarawi right now," Yia-yia says. There is steel in her voice. "We will get this sorted out."

"No!" I exclaim, clutching at her arm. "That's probably just what Matt wants. I'll look like I'm overreacting. My shirt *was* untucked, and it's only my word against Matt's that he's targeting me specifically. Maybe I'm wrong," I say. "Maybe it was just a coincidence."

There is another moment of quiet as Yia-yia considers this.

"This Matt Spader." Lil's icy voice comes from the back seat. "Does he have any particular phobias that we know of? Snakes? Spiders?"

"Where are you going to get snakes from?" I snort.

"I have my methods," Lil says.

"Well, I don't need you slipping snakes into his sports bag, or Yia-yia talking to the teachers," I say, straightening my shoulders.

"I was thinking his lunch box would be most effective." Lil chuckles evilly. "Spider sandwiches, anyone?"

"I'm going to handle this myself," I say, choosing to ignore this. "Matt Spader will be sorry he ever messed with me." I lift my chin. "And I'm not alone. I have my friends to help me. We'll come up with something, we always do."

Yia-yia gives me a long look. "I have no doubt that you can do anything you set your mind to, Effie," she says finally, "but I would still like you to talk to a teacher." She interrupts my protest with a wave of her hand. "It does not have to be the head teacher, just a grown-up that you trust. I think you will feel better if someone at the school knows what is going on. I know I will."

I think this over for a moment. "OK," I say finally. "I'll try and talk to Mr Jameson. He's in charge of student council at the moment. I'm sure if I can just make him see how Matt's abusing the prefect system then he'll do something about it." I start to feel better as I think this over.

"Good." Yia-yia pushes the sunglasses back up her nose. "And now, I think we could all use an adventure!"

I pester her to tell me where we're going, but she just shakes her head mysteriously. We drive for a while, singing show tunes and playing I spy.

We get further out of town, winding through country lanes, and I start to feel better. Sometimes having a big cry is like when a thunderstorm clears the air, leaving it all cool and crisp. That's what my brain is like now – cool and crisp. The further away we get from the school the more I can see that Matt's attempts to bully me are actually pretty desperate. By the time we turn sharply on to a long gravel driveway, I'm feeling more like myself. It seems like Yia-yia's kidnapping efforts were perfectly timed.

"Where are we?" I ask as we glide slowly down the drive. Just then we round a corner and a ginormous house appears. It's long and low and covered in ivy. It's even got a little turret like something in a fairy tale.

Yia-yia stops the car and climbs out. A man in a

smart uniform appears instantly at her side and takes the keys from her hand, then he holds the back door open so that Lil can get out.

"Thank you, Parker," Lil says as she sweeps past him into the house. "That will be all."

I scuttle out after her and in through the shining doors. "How did you know his name?" I hiss.

Lil shrugs. "I didn't, but he looked like a Parker, don't you think?"

I roll my eyes, but I'm already distracted, taking in the scene in front of me. Across the polished marble floor, an equally polished woman, wearing the same red lipstick as Yia-yia, stands behind a huge shining desk.

"Cucumber water?" she asks softly, gesturing to a tray of glasses and a big jug.

"Um, thanks," I mutter, pouring a glass.

"Yia-yia!" I whisper, slurping on the cucumber water (weirdly nice). "Where are we?"

Yia-yia raises her sunglasses, perching them on top of her head. "We're at a spa, of course," she says. She turns towards the lady at the reception desk. "We have a booking under 'Kostas'," she says.

The woman taps on the keyboard in front of her with long red fingernails. "I've found you," she says.

"Welcome. Afternoon tea and three pamper packages?"

"That's right." Yia-yia nods. "I am treating my extraordinary granddaughters." She gestures towards us proudly and then waits, as though she expects a round of applause for having such excellent taste in grandchildren. The woman smiles.

"How nice," she says. "If you'd like to follow Anna, she'll take you through to the treatment rooms."

It seems like only five minutes later we are sitting in reclining chairs, with delicious-smelling mush spread on our faces, and our feet in little baths with rose petals floating on the top.

"This is the life," Lil sighs happily. "Now tell me. Does Matt Spader keep his lunch box in his locker?"

CHAPTER *Seventeen*

I have at times been called "highly strung" (I myself prefer words like "spirited" or "passionate") but after an hour of having my feet soaked and my nails painted with sparkly purple nail varnish and my face coated in gloop that looks like blueberry yogurt, followed by tea with cucumber sandwiches, slabs of Victoria sponge AND scones with strawberry jam and thick dollops of clotted cream (jam first, of course) even I am finding it hard not be relaxed. I have even almost forgotten about Matt Spader.

Almost.

We exit the spa wearing matching giant sunglasses, Lil slipping a shiny pound coin into the-man-who-is-not-really-called-Parker's hand as she passes him.

"Thanks, Yia-yia," I sigh, sliding bonelessly into my seat. "I'm so chilled I feel like a tub of mint choc chip." (Everyone knows mint choc chip is the chilliest of ice creams.)

"It is always good to look after yourself," Yia-yia says, smoothing back her hair.

"That's why I've been so mellow since I started doing my meditation," Lil agrees, pulling a notebook out of her backpack with the words MY ENEMIES emblazoned on it. She carefully adds Matt Spader to the top of what looks like a worryingly long list.

I crane my neck to read. "Does that say *Mary Berry*?" I ask.

"She knows what she did," Lil says.

I grin. I'm in such a good mood, it's almost, *almost* like the horrible afternoon didn't happen.

Dad helps Lil unpack her school bag while she fills him in on the afternoon and wiggles her toes about to show off the paint on her nails (a dazzling mix of rainbow glitter). I check my phone and notice I have twelve increasingly frantic messages from Angelika wanting to know if I'm OK. I send a quick reply letting her know I'm feeling much better and I include a chain of my most positive emojis to really make sure she knows I'm telling the truth.

"Thanks again, Yia-yia," I say. "It really did help."

"What are grandparents for?" Yia-yia smiles, sinking into the sofa. "Dimitri?" she calls regally. "Where is my tea? All this relaxation is rather exhausting."

I don't feel at all tired. It's like my brain has quietened down so that I can think clearly. I'm ready for action. I pound up the stairs to my bedroom, hit play on the *Hamilton* soundtrack, sit down on my bed and, as the Schuyler sisters sing about being part of history, I decide to make a plan. I have found that everything is better when you have a plan.

I turn to a fresh page of my notebook and select a gold sparkly pen. Then I begin to write:

PLAN TO DEFEAT MATT SPADER

1. Talk to Mr J. Get to the bottom of how Matt has rigged the prefect selection. It surely can't be a coincidence that ALL his friends are prefects???!!!
2. Arrange interview with school paper – expose Matt's corruption to the masses, AND get our GREEN DEAL message out.
3. Organize the bake sale. Make a sign-up sheet for

the river clean-up, talk to students and spread
the word. We need to get this moving!!!!

I look at the list with satisfaction. Matt might be a
villain, but there's plenty I can do to fight him. Lying
back against my pillows, I feel a smile spread across
my face. I can't believe that I ever let that dumb
boy get in my head. Tomorrow, I think, I'll turn
everything around.

CHAPTER *Eighteen*

It's the next day, and things are not going to plan AT ALL.

First thing, I bump into Matt and his pal Andrew.

"Running in the corridor, Ellie?" Matt tuts.

"I wasn't running in the corridor," I snap. "I was walking briskly and with purpose. *You* are the one who barged into *me*."

Matt makes a tsking sound. "I don't know, Andy," he sighs. "What do you think?" He shoots his friend a wink, and a slow smile spreads across Andy's face.

"Oh, yeah," he says, pulling out a notebook. "Definitely running in the corridor." It's then that I notice the prefect badge, and with a sinking heart I realize where this is going.

"That's a demerit, then, isn't it?" Matt sighs elaborately. "For Effie Kostas."

"Oh, *now* you remember my name!" I hiss as Andy writes it down.

Andy ambles off, leaving me and Matt alone.

"So I was right," I say, trying to keep my voice steady. "Your prefects are targeting me."

"I don't know what you're talking about." Matt's eyes widen innocently.

"I wasn't running," I say. "You *know* I wasn't running."

"It's not up to me. It's the prefects who decide if someone's breaking the rules." Matt sticks his hands in his pockets and shrugs.

"How strange that all the prefects just happen to be your best friends," I mutter darkly.

"That was a coincidence, wasn't it?"

"I don't think it was a coincidence."

Matt's smile slips at that. "I don't know what you're suggesting. . ."

"I'm SUGGESTING that you rigged the selection."

"My, my, what an imagination you have." His smile is back, and wider now. He pauses for a second. "Even IF I did, what do *you* think you could do about it?"

"I'll tell people," I say, trying to keep my voice steady. "I'll tell them you rigged the selection and that you're using the prefects to do your dirty work."

For a second Matt's blue eyes are as cold as ice. "Do you really think this school will believe *you* over me? Why don't you just keep your nose out of it? Otherwise you might find out what people really think of you."

I stand there, stunned, as he turns and walks away. I search my brain for a good comeback. But no words come, and I'm left standing in the corridor, a cold sense of dread in my chest.

CHAPTER *Nineteen*

I refuse to let Matt scare me, so during lunch I corner Mr Jameson in his classroom and explain the whole thing.

He doesn't react how I thought he would. "I'm sorry, Effie," he says. "I see no reason to interfere with a system that seems perfectly acceptable to me."

I stare at him, speechless. I laid out the problems with Matt's prefect programme. I used statistics! There were graphs! I put together an entire page of inspirational quotes from world leaders on the importance of fairly elected officials! How is it possible that Mr Jameson has not been moved?

Mr Jameson sighs. "I understand there is some friction between you and Matt. Something about your unsuccessful run for student council. . ."

"That's got nothing to do with anything!" I leap in, feeling my cheeks heat up. "I just want the prefect selection to be fair."

"And it was fair," Mr Jameson says. "I oversaw the selection process myself. There was nothing untoward there."

"How did it work?" I ask, insistent.

He sighs again. "Matt and I whittled the list down to fifteen candidates based on their school records and contribution to extracurricular activities."

"So all of the football team got in," I point out.

"Yes, among others." Mr Jameson nods. "Then we wrote all those names down on pieces of paper and pulled them out of a hat."

"Who wrote them down?" I ask.

"Matt did," Mr Jameson says reluctantly.

"And who pulled them out?"

Mr Jameson thinks about it for a second. "I believe Matt did."

"AHA!" I leap to my feet like I'm Poirot. "J'ACCUSE!!!!! So Matt could *easily* have marked the papers he wanted and then picked them out?"

Mr Jameson looks at me like I've grown an extra head. "Effie, these conspiracy theories are becoming ridiculous. There's absolutely no need to become hysterical over something like this."

"I'm not hysterical!" I exclaim.

"Look." Mr Jameson leans back in his chair and gestures at his desk. "I have an enormous stack of marking to do. I was hoping for a quiet lunch break to get on with it. I really don't have time for these personal squabbles."

"This isn't—" I start, but Mr Jameson cuts me off with a sweep of his hand.

"You are the only person to complain about this, Effie," he says. "And as far as I'm aware, the only person who has a problem with Matt filling in as president while Aaron is off ill. Losing is hard, but as you get older you have to learn that not everything will go your way."

"But . . . but, I'm *right*," I say desperately.

Teachers are supposed to be there to help. Mr Jameson is talking to me like I'm a toddler having a tantrum, and I'm embarrassed to feel tears stinging the backs of my eyes.

Mr Jameson obviously notices because his voice becomes VERY kind as he says, "Now, Effie, I know everything feels like the end of the world at your age, but trust me, this will all blow over."

There doesn't seem to be anything else to say. I

shuffle outside, where Angelika is waiting for me.

"How did it go?" she asks. Then she sees my face and wraps her arm around my shoulders. "What happened?"

In flat tones I lay out the conversation for her. I can actually feel her vibrating with anger next to me. "Let's go back in there together," she says. "Maybe the two of us can convince him."

I shake my head. "It will just look even worse," I say. "You're my best friend, of course you'd be on my side. He thinks it's just a fight between me and Matt, he doesn't understand that it's so much bigger. Matt using the fundraising money for his own stupid football uniforms, giving his friends special privileges. Abandoning the recycling programme and the river clean-up."

"OK, so number one on your list didn't work," Angelika says after a moment. "But that wasn't the only thing on there. We can use the bake sale at the fete to talk to students about the river clean-up. We can go to the paper and do an interview explaining what's going on. Once the truth is out there then more people will stand up against Matt and the teachers will HAVE to do something."

"I know," I say. "I'm just angry."

"I understand." Angelika nods. "I am too. But just remember, Matt's only the acting president. In a couple of weeks his reign of terror will be over and things will go back to normal."

"You're right," I say. "Next step, the free press. Thank goodness there's still one way to get the truth out there."

CHAPTER *Twenty*

EXCLUSIVE:
EFFIE KOSTAS
TROUBLED TEEN OR SORE LOSER?

By Catriona McGiddens

In an **EXCLUSIVE** interview, this reporter met with Effie Kostas, to dish on her failed bid for school council president – and her recent erratic behaviour.

Cutting straight to the heart of the matter like a hot journalistic knife through butter, I ask Effie what was behind the latest scene in the canteen in which a prefect was **FORCED** to

Why, I ask, is Effie on a personal crusade to bring down acting president Matt Spader? Surely he deserves our support? Is it a case of **SOUR GRAPES** after having lost out in her own

THIS KIND OF OUT-OF-CONTROL TEMPER IS CLEARLY WHAT IS CAUSING TROUBLE FOR THE CURRENT ADMINISTRATION.

hand her a demerit.

Effie mutters that it was a mistake – but can't deny the demerit was justified. What does Effie say to those who call her a troublemaker?

"If standing up for myself and what I believe in makes me a troublemaker, then I guess that they're right," Miss Kostas answers hotly.

bid for student president?

"I was gutted to lose," she admits. "But that doesn't mean I can't care or have an opinion. I might not be the president, but I'm a student, I'm part of the community that the council is supposed to represent, and if I think what they're doing is wrong then I have to speak up and say so. We all do."

So it's not all a bit ... personal? "It's **NOT** personal," Effie protests. "Matt Spader is abusing his position as acting president. He's created his own little army of prefects, chosen from his friends, and he's using them to target people who oppose him."

QUITE THE ACCUSATION!!!! It certainly seems as though Effie has a grudge against our new president, flinging wild conspiracy theories around.

"Aaron and I wanted to make the fete a green event," Effie goes on. "To raise money for a river clean-up and launch our recycling campaign. Matt threw all those plans out so that he could play paintball and raise money for new football shirts. That is **NOT** a good use of funds."

It seems that other students would disagree. "That Effie girl seems weird," one student said in response. "Plus, what's wrong with paintball? She just wants to stop anyone having any fun."

Is this the end of Effie's disruptive behaviour? Or does she have more in store for our rightfully elected government? With the school fete **ONLY DAYS AWAY** I guess we'll all find out soon enough...

CHAPTER *Twenty-One*

I whack the newspaper down on the table in front of me.

"Stop reading it!" Angelika exclaims.

"Yeah," Jess adds. "You're not going to change what it says."

It's the day of the school fete and we're setting up our bake sale booth near the school gates. It's cold and overcast, but it's not raining.

"I can't believe Matt's got Catriona on his side as well," I say, my voice small and tight like a clenched fist. "This article is a joke. She didn't include any of the stuff I told her about the Green Deal."

"At least she included that bit about you standing up for what you believe in," Kevin says comfortingly.

"Only so she could call me a troublemaker!" I huff in frustration.

"You've read it a million times in the last couple of days," Angelika puts in. "It's a stupid article and you shouldn't waste your energy on it."

"I just don't understand," I say bleakly. "First Mr Jameson won't listen to me, and now the school newspaper – which is supposed to INFORM students, to TELL THE TRUTH – is trying to make me look like an idiot. How can things be so ... so ... WRONG?"

"It's messed up," Ruby says. "If you want me to have a word with Catriona McGiddens then I'd be HAPPY to do it."

"And add 'intimidating journalists' to Matt's accusations?" I snort. "Yeah, *that* would go down well."

"It wouldn't be intimidation." Ruby smiles coolly, glancing at her fingernails. "It would be ... a conversation." I'm reminded again why Ruby is Lil's hero.

"Ugh! Kevin, what ARE these?" We're interrupted by Jess, who is wrinkling up her nose at the contents of a Tupperware box she's just opened.

"They're Mum's gluten-free, dairy-free, sugar-free mung bean biscuits." Kevin sighs. "They're actually not her worst effort. You get used to them . . . sort of."

"Just put them at the back," I say hastily. I still want the bake sale to be a success. It makes me sick that we're raising money for Matt's stupid uniforms, but at least we can try and sign people up for the river clean-up at the same time. "We all did such a good job on biscuit decorating!" I say, making my voice extra cheery. "I think it was the right call to go for animals rather than rubbish in the end."

"Yeah," Jess agrees. "That biscuit in the shape of an overflowing bin you made looked disgusting."

"I can't help it if my art is TOO convincing," I say.

"These ones that are a tribute to Feathers will sell especially well," Kevin puts in, carefully setting out the pigeon-shaped biscuits. "He truly was a bird in a million."

We all bow our heads for a moment in a gesture of respect. That pigeon certainly won over a lot of hearts before he flew into that window.

"Remember," I say firmly, "our main job today is to sign people up for the river clean-up."

We finish setting up the stand and put the donations tin on the table.

"Football uniforms," Ruby snorts, echoing my thoughts. "I can't believe we're helping Matt Spader buy T-shirts that flatter his eyes."

"Oh, hello, Ellie." A voice reaches my ears. A terrible, obnoxious, awful voice. Speak of the devil. I swing round and there's Matt Spader. He is – unbelievably – wearing actual camouflage gear, like he's stepped out of *Call of Duty*. "Good of you to come," he says. "I wasn't sure you'd turn up."

"You should know I don't break a promise," I say. "I said I'd be here and I am. No poorly researched, biased article is going to stop me."

"Whoa, whoa, whoa." Matt holds his hands up. "I thought the article was very fair. And that's what I told Catriona when we were hanging out at the weekend." His face is so smug it's almost unbearable.

"You might have the teachers and the school paper in your pocket," I grind out, "but we'll find a way to make sure the students know who you really are."

Just then a car pulls up and a couple of boys get out. They call over to Matt and all three of them do a noisy and elaborate handshake.

"Paintball time!" one of the boys says. "Great idea, man."

"I'll be right behind you," Matt says as the two boys wander through the gates. "Looks like the rest of the students seem to like me just fine," he says, turning back to me. "Which is more than I can say for you. This bake sale's not exactly a great success so far, is it? I do hope you're not going to let the school down . . . again."

"It's going to be a success," Angelika chimes in hotly.

"Yeah." Ruby folds her arms across her chest and eyes Matt up and down. "And you're standing in the way of our customers."

"My apologies." Matt smiles that smile that doesn't reach his eyes. "I'll buy a biscuit to make up for it, shall I? How about this one. What's it supposed to be? A turtle?"

"That," Kevin spits out, "is Feathers the pigeon. Show some respect."

Matt drops a pound coin into the tin, where it rattles loudly. Then he bites into the biscuit, taking off the head in one neat mouthful.

"All right, Matt," a voice calls. It's another one of Matt's friends. He's also wearing stupid camouflage, and he has his prefect badge pinned to the front of his shirt.

"Dave! Just in time," Matt says. "I'm afraid I just saw Effie here littering." He shakes his head sadly.

"What?!" My eyebrows snap up.

"Oh no," Dave says. "Littering on school grounds?

That's a demerit."

"I didn't litter!" I exclaim. "I would NEVER. He's making it up. Where is this alleged litter?"

"I put it in the bin, of course," Matt says smoothly. "Another demerit, Effie." He tuts. "That means you've had three this week. And you know what *that* means."

I feel the blood drain from my face. "You can't be serious?" I hiss through clenched teeth.

"Automatic detention."

"DETENTION?!" I burst out. I've never, never had detention before. Will this go on some sort of permanent record? Will it stop me being prime minister one day? "I didn't do it!" I wheeze.

"I saw you," Matt says with a shrug. "So did Dave. Didn't you, Dave?"

Dave nods. "Afraid so," he says.

"It was me who dropped the litter." Zo steps forward suddenly. "Not Effie."

Matt's eyes flick over her. She flinches a little, but she stands her ground.

"No, it was me," Angelika pipes up.

"I did it," Ruby says.

"No one did it," Jess says. "But if they did ... it was me."

"It was me!" Kevin cries, holding his hands out as

if to be arrested. "Lock me up, officer."

Matt glares at the group for a moment. "Fine," he says, his voice as cold as ice. "If you all want detention, then that can be arranged."

"You can't do this!" I yell. "I won't let you."

"Shall I get Mr Jameson?" Matt asks, lifting one eyebrow. "We can see what he says." He smiles. "I thought not. And I'm afraid I'll have to bring someone else in to run the bake sale. Under the circumstances I don't think we can trust a bunch of kids that have disciplinary issues with school funds."

"You won't get away with this." My voice shakes a little. "Aaron will be back soon, and then your little reign of terror will be over."

Matt smiles again, and this time his eyes glitter in a way that makes me feel nervous. "Oh, didn't you know? If an acting president is in place for over four weeks, he becomes president permanently. I'm surprised you weren't aware of that particular fact. It's in the school rules you're so fond of."

"W-what?" I manage.

"That's right. And we all know that Aaron's dad wants him off until he's fully recovered. Your little eco-warrior days are over."

"Aaron won't let you do that!" I exclaim.

"Aaron's totally cool with it," Matt replies. "We had a chat the other day. He thinks I'll do a great job. He's got way bigger things to worry about at the moment."

We all stare at him in silence.

"Hey, Matt." Katie suddenly appears at his elbow, wearing her prefect badge. She completely ignores me and my friends. I try not to let it hurt my feelings, but it feels like just one more jab in a fight I'm losing. "Are we paintballing or not?" she asks.

"Yeah, we are," Matt says, slinging his arm around her shoulder. "See you later, Ellie. Enjoy detention."

CHAPTER Twenty-Two

The next day finds us all in detention.

I don't really know what I expected detention to be like. Maybe more like prison. I thought there'd be bars on the window and a jailer with jangling keys on his belt, and a stale slice of bread shoved through a slot for us to gnaw on. I thought there'd be more rats and possibly that we'd have to join a gang to survive.

Instead, it's just us, after everyone has got home, and we're sitting in the library with a teacher called Mrs Watson. I try, again, to tell her that we don't belong here, that we've done nothing wrong. She tells me, rather wearily, to sit down, and that detention is time for silent study.

I sit at my desk and open my maths textbook, but

the numbers just blur in front of my eyes. How can this be happening? I can't even bring myself to look at my friends, who are all here because they stuck up for me.

When I was running against Aaron we disagreed and we fought, but at least there were rules that I understood. What chance do I have against Matt? He's not just ignoring the rules. He's the one making them.

It's not very often that I don't know what to do, but I am totally stuck now. I tried talking to a grown-up, I tried talking to the newspaper. Nothing worked. Matt even had us thrown off the bake sale so that we couldn't sign people up to the river clean-up. Everything on my list failed. It all feels hopeless. And now we're in detention! I told my dad that I was going to Angelika's after school because I didn't even know how to explain it to him.

Mrs Watson gets to her feet.

"I have some work to do in the computer lab," she says. "I will be back in to check on you and I don't want to find you talking or messing around. Is that understood?"

"Yes, miss," we all mutter dutifully, and she goes out.

There's a moment of quiet, till we're sure she's really gone, and then Ruby heaves an enormous sigh.

"Well," she says. "I guess Matt Spader has declared war."

Kevin nods. "He's obviously targeting us."

I look up at them. "I'm so sorry, you guys. I dragged you into this."

"Effie, this is NOT your fault," Ruby says hotly.

"No one dragged us," Jess says. "We all think what Matt is doing is wrong."

They're all on their feet now, surrounding my desk. Zo gives me an encouraging smile. Angelika wraps an arm around my shoulder. I start to feel a tiny bit better. I love my friends.

That's when I feel the first sparks of anger. It's one thing going after me, but now Matt is messing with my friends.

"I think it says a lot about how dangerous Matt thinks you are," Angelika says, interrupting my thoughts. "He's obviously worried that you really will be able to convince the school he's up to no good. That's why he's doing this. Getting in first, so that people won't believe you."

As Angelika's words settle, those sparks build into a burning and extremely RIGHTEOUS anger. I think I am actually vibrating with fury. If I was the Incredible Hulk I'd be twenty feet tall right now and as green as a giant pea.

"You're right," I say.

"He truly is an evil genius," Kevin says.

"Yeah, Matt Spader ... more like DARTH SPADER," Ruby says.

Kevin laughs and his pencil starts whipping across the page.

Ruby's right. It is starting to feel like we're in a story like *Star Wars*, one where the school is suddenly under the control of an EMPIRE OF DARKNESS.

But the Empire didn't win, despite being more powerful. That's when I realize something. I need to stop playing by the rules. Sometimes you have to fight fire with fire.

"We need to be the rebels!" I say, jumping to my feet. My friends all look confused.

"Like in Star Wars," I explain. "If Matt really is part of the awful empire of oppression, we've got to be the rebel alliance. We have to start a resistance!"

"That's more like it!" Angelika grins. "I was starting to worry about you."

"So what do we do?" Kevin asks.

I hesitate. "I'm not sure you guys should help," I say. "This means fighting dirty. I might do more stuff that gets me in trouble or in detention. I can't ask you to do that. It has to be my fight."

"Well, that's dumb." Ruby crosses her arms across her chest. "Sorry, Effie, but we can make up our own minds. I'm not going anywhere."

"Me neither," Jess says staunchly, and the others murmur in agreement.

"We're ALL here because of Matt," Angelika reminds me. "We all want to help bring him down."

"OK," I say finally. "But if we have to do something that breaks the rules and you don't want to, just say. I know that not everyone can always afford to get in trouble. Everyone understand?" They all nod, solemnly.

"So, now that's decided," Kevin says. "What *do*

we do now?"

I do have one idea of where to start. "I know the first person I'd want to talk to about being a rebel," I grin. "Iris!"

"YES," Ruby agrees. "She'll have all her activist wisdom to share."

"Yep," I say. "I'll go and see her after this and see if she has any suggestions."

"I'll go with you," Angelika says. "I have another idea as well." She walks over to her desk, flips through her notebook and takes out a sheet of paper. "Matt says he can take over the presidency full-time because it's in the school rules. I looked carefully at the rules this afternoon, and what he said is true. No one can run against him either."

I groan. "BUT," Angelika continues with a little grin, "there CAN be a vote of no confidence. If we call for it, Ms Shaarawi has to let us have one. Then if enough people come out to vote to say they think Matt is doing a bad job, he gets removed from his position."

"So we'd have to get a majority to vote against him?" I ask.

"That's right. The majority of the junior school, which means we need at least two hundred and fifty votes. If people don't vote at all it counts for Matt."

"Who would be the president then?" Jess asks. "If he did get voted out?"

"The council would run without a president until the original president came back or the next election, whichever is soonest."

"So if we can convince enough people to vote, Aaron would be able to come back?" I ask. If you'd told me a few months ago how happy that would make me, I would never have believed you.

Angelika nods, and the rest of the group cheer. Thank goodness for my best friend. The girl's a genius.

"If Aaron actually *wants* to come back, that is," Kevin says suddenly. "Matt said that Aaron was over council now. He might not want to be president any more."

"We'll cross that bridge when we come to it," I say, with a confidence I don't feel.

"First things first, we have to get Ms Shaarawi to set up the vote. Then we HAVE to find a way to help our fellow students see the truth about Matt before it takes place. Agreed?"

"Agreed," they all chime.

"Down with Darth Spader!" Kevin holds up the drawing he's been working on with a flourish.

"Kevin!" I say. "That is brilliant."

It really is. It's a picture of Matt Spader wearing a Darth Vader helmet and his stupid football uniform. Underneath him are all of us – Zo, Kevin, Ruby, Jess, Angelika and me – standing in a group pose holding lightsabres.

We all gather round. "We are the resistance," I say. "We'll find a way to save the school from Matt's evil clutches." I draw myself up to my full height. "We're going to fight back. We're going to be the rebels."

They nod solemnly, and Jess bows her head. "May the force be with us," she says.

CHAPTER *Twenty-Three*

I'm still feeling a sense of purpose and burning enthusiasm when I knock on Iris's door after detention.

"Oh, it's you, is it?' Iris sniffs as she shuffles away from the door and towards her kitchen.

Angelika and I follow her through. It might not sound like an enthusiastic welcome, but the freshly baked fruit cake that gets pulled out and placed in front of us in Iris's hot pink kitchen tells a different story.

"YOU DAFT CARROT STICK!" Lennon, Iris's parrot, seems to feel differently.

"Hello, Lennon, you *głupi idiota*," Angelika says affectionately. She's trying to expand Lennon's rude vocabulary to include some Polish insults. Iris is very encouraging.

"WHAT A POTATO," Lennon says darkly, which leads me to believe he can dish it out but not take it.

"*Ziemniak*," Angelika corrects him. "*Co za ziemniak.*"

Iris pulls out mugs and cuts us enormous slices of cake with slightly shaky hands, before levering herself into a seat.

"So," she says, "did you two just come to corrupt my parrot and eat my cake?"

"Sounds like a pretty good afternoon to me," I say. "But actually, we came to ask for your help." I take a bite of cake. There are extra cherries in it – my favourite, as Iris knows.

"Oh yes?" Iris looks over the top of her mug. "What can I help you with?"

"We need to know how to lead a resistance movement," I say.

"And we thought you were the right person to ask," Angelika adds.

Iris gives one of her rare grins. It scrunches up her whole face, and her eyes twinkle happily.

"Well, well." She chuckles and leans back in her chair. "What brought this on?"

"Well." I lean forward. "Things have definitely got a lot worse since we last spoke. . ."

"The main problem," Angelika puts in, "is

Matt Spader."

She says the words like they are one of Lennon's worst insults.

"Maybe the worst human being in existence," I add.

"He's got some tough competition," Iris says thoughtfully. "So, this Matt is a problem?"

Angelika nods. "We'd better start from the beginning."

We tell Iris the whole story, about Matt rigging the prefect selection and using them to target us. About the hopeless teachers, and the corruption at the school paper. We tell her about the vote of no confidence loophole, and how we have one last chance to stop Matt from becoming the permanent president and destroying the school with his awful policies, but we don't know how to get the truth out there.

"What you're saying is that official channels are not working." Iris's eyes gleam. "You need to go outside the law."

"Well, maybe not outside the *law*," I say doubtfully, and Iris looks disappointed. "But outside the Highworth Grange Secondary School chain of command."

"Good enough." Iris taps her fingers on the table. "And you need a way to get your story out there."

"Exactly," I agree.

"I know just where you should start," Iris says. "Have you two ever heard of zines?"

"*Zeens?*" I repeat.

"*Zines*, as in maga*zines*," Iris says. "They're handmade. You cut pictures and letters out of magazines and newspapers and things and stick them into a booklet, then you photocopy the booklet and hand them out. They're the perfect way to get information out."

"That sounds like it could work," I say.

"Imagine the potential stationery-buying opportunities," Angelika breathes.

"We've used them in lots of different ways over the years." Iris's eyes cloud over with the memories. "In fact I probably have a few knocking about. I'll dig them out for you if you've got a few minutes." She eyes the plate in front of us – now empty apart from a few meagre crumbs. "And I suppose I'd better find some more cake. Anyone would think you two didn't get fed at home."

Iris finds us some of the zines she worked on and they're amazing. They're like proper works of art. They really say something. The ones Iris shows us are mostly about women's rights and they're full of artwork and poetry and beautiful, stirring words.

Finally, Iris tells us it's getting late, and Angelika and I tear ourselves away and hustle back to my house for dinner.

"Those zines were so cool," Angelika says after we've finished. We are lounging on the floor in my room with Lil, flicking through Netflix and dunking fizzy worms in chocolate milk.

"Mmmm," I agree. I can feel the squiggly feeling of excitement running through me at the thought of making one ourselves. "I think it could be the perfect way to make our voices heard. We can talk about the Green Deal, and we can advertise the river clean-up, AND we can write about what Matt's doing."

"I hope it helps with the fundraising efforts," Angelika says. "At the moment we've only managed to raise about seven pounds in the donation box."

"And five of those were from my pocket money," I add glumly.

"I've been thinking about leading a rebellion myself, actually," Lil interrupts then. "Have you noticed that Mum and Dad seem a bit TOO keen to get me to eat my peas?"

I chuckle, and Lil glowers from under her eyebrows. "I'm serious," she insists. "I think it's a conspiracy."

"I think they're just conspiring to get you to eat some vitamins," I say.

"There's real fruit juice in these jelly worms," Lil says. "It says so on the packet." She frowns. "They probably have money invested in pea farms or something."

"Big pea money." Angelika nods wisely.

There's a pause and then all three of us dissolve into giggles.

"Right, you lot." Mum's head pokes around the door then, her crackling cloud of dark hair almost as wild as my own. "That's enough merriment for a school night. Angelika, your mum's here to pick you up."

After Angelika leaves I go to my room and lie on my bed, staring up at the ceiling. My mind is whirring and I try to concentrate on taking deep breaths, like Lil told me to. Suddenly it seems like there's a lot to do, a lot to organize, and even a born leader like myself can feel overwhelmed at times.

I look at the pictures that are stuck up on my wall, pictures of people I find inspiring, from Vanessa Nakate to David Attenborough. They all had to start somewhere and I will start here. Protecting my school from a villain – and helping Highworth Grange to finally go green.

139

CHAPTER *Twenty-Four*

The next day we meet in our campaign office to fill the rest of the gang in on what Iris had to say, and we show them the zine that Iris let us borrow. The whole group are really enthusiastic. Kevin is especially keen.

"This is so cool," he says, leafing through the zine in his hands. "I can't believe this artwork. It's such an amazing way of making something . . . like, it's so low tech."

I nod. "I already asked Mum if we could use the photocopier at her work. I told her it was for a school project."

"Oooh, Effie the rebel strikes already," Ruby teases. "'School project.'" She puts little air quotes around the words with her fingers. "You liar."

I grin. "Well, it *is* a project *for* the school," I say. "It's not exactly a lie. Plus we have to be as stealthy as possible."

"Effie and I were thinking we should have a name for our group – one that we can use on the zine. So that we can be a bit more anonymous," Angelika adds.

"If we use my name on anything Matt will just say it's personal again," I say.

"What about the Highworth Grange Eco-Warriors?" Angelika suggests.

"Oooh, I like it," I say.

"We sound FIERCE," Kevin puts in.

"Like, if you want to mess with Mother Nature you've got to go through us first!" Ruby poses like a superhero.

We're all laughing when the door bursts open. I freeze as Matt Spader glides into the room. Even the way he moves is like a villain, all slippery and skulking.

"I thought I'd find you all hiding in here," he says, looking at us like we're bugs that he's tempted to tread on.

Unfortunately, I am currently sitting on the purple beanbag, and – as I've already mentioned – it's not the ideal position from which to rise gracefully in order to confront your mortal enemy. After a bit of squishing and huffing and rolling on my side, I leap to my feet and toss my head, smoothing my hair down with one hand.

"Matt," I say finally, with all the disdain I can muster.

"Quite the display, Effie," he drawls. "Such natural grace. You should think about trying out for the gymnastics team."

"Effie is not very good at gymnastics," Jess points out.

"Yes, thanks, Jess," I say, as Matt starts to smirk.

"But she's really good at lots of other things," Jess continues. "You're not good at many things. You're not even that good at football. You're sort of medium at football."

Matt's smirk slips.

"Whatever," he says icily. "I just wanted to drop in to say nice work on this whole vote of no confidence thing."

"Oh, you heard about that, did you?" I allow a cool smile to spread across my face. "It seems someone wrote an anonymous letter to Ms Shaarawi pointing out that the acting student president couldn't just *waltz* into the job permanently without THE PEOPLE actually having a say about it."

"Good for them," Matt says. Something in his expression worries me – he looks far too pleased with himself. "Far be it for me to deny people a chance to vote me in."

"Oh, they won't be voting you in..." Angelika pipes up.

"They'll be voting you *out*," Ruby and Kevin say at the same time. They grin at each other and high five.

I don't say anything. Why is Matt still smirking?

"Well, I guess we'll see at the vote, won't we?" Matt says. "A week on Saturday."

"A week on Saturday?!" I exclaim. "But that's the first weekend of the holidays. No one will be at school!"

"They can always come in to vote," Matt says. "If they really want to."

It's another second before the full horror of it all dawns on me. "*And* that's the weekend of the river clean-up," I groan.

"Oh dear, is it?" Matt opens his eyes wide. "Your little pet project. What a shame. Well, to be honest I don't think anyone will be making either event. Not when they've all been invited to a pizza party at my house on that day."

I can feel the tension crank up in the small room. I don't say anything, just look steadily at this boy, my mortal enemy. Are there any lengths he won't go to? And why must my nemeses keep using pizza against me?? I love pizza!

"Yup. Pizza, gaming. My dad's going to hire a DJ. Of course, you'll still be able to vote, I suppose," Matt says, one final twist of the knife. "After all, none of you are invited." With that he gives a cheery wave of his hand and disappears out the door.

"Effie?" Angelika's voice is almost a whisper. "Are you OK?"

My breathing is hard. I'm struggling to contain all the anger that's inside me. It feels like I've swallowed a fireball, like I could open my mouth and just start shooting fireballs at people. Which would be amazing.

"I'm OK," I manage finally, my voice a little raspy. "In fact, I'm better than OK." I spin around to face my friends, adrenaline singing through me. "Look at all the trouble Matt's going to just to keep the vote from happening. He KNOWS we can beat him. And we will. He won't get away with this. . . Not on our watch."

CHAPTER *Twenty-Five*

"OK," Angelika says, her hands on her hips. "I've organized the room into various different stations."

She gestures at each small pile of supplies neatly placed around her bedroom. We decided to all meet up together over the weekend to work on the zine. Everyone is getting their own page to do. After our run-in with Matt yesterday it all feels even more urgent. We've got a lot of stuff we need to say.

The really good thing is how something like this lets all of us feel creative. Kevin is so artistic that I know his pages will look amazing, and he's in charge of the cover. The rest of us can all cut and stick things – even I, with my total lack of artistic skills, can cope with that. The page I'm in charge of is a letter to our fellow students, and you'd better believe I'm going to make it as stirring as possible.

"Newspapers and magazines for cutting up over there, felt tip pens and Sharpies over there. Glue and glitter glue here, paper of assorted size and colour there. Now, does everyone have scissors?"

"Yes, Angelika," we chorus, standing to attention like troops ready for inspection.

"Very good." Angelika nods briskly. "Then we can begin."

"I'd forgotten what you're like in organization mode," Ruby grins. "Fierce."

"These biscuits are so good," Kevin groans, munching on the little ginger cookies filled with jam that Angelika's mum brought up to her room. "My mum's still on her health kick," he says glumly. "We had to eat pizza made out of cauliflower last night."

Zo pats his shoulder gently.

"How was that?" Angelika asks.

"How do you think it was?" Kevin says sadly. "It was pizza MADE OUT OF CAULIFLOWER."

"Sounds disgusting," Jess agrees cheerfully. "Have another biscuit."

We all focus then and start cutting bits of paper.

"Everything all right, Effie?" Ruby asks, glancing over.

"Fine," I say. "Why do you ask?"

"Maybe something to do with the words you've cut out." Jess points to the little pile of words I've cut out in front of me.

NIGHTMARE

ENEMY

DISASTER

WEASEL

I sigh. "I can't stop thinking about how Matt's trying to scam all the other students."

"Matt Spader really *is* a nightmare-enemy-disaster-weasel," Angelika says firmly.

Ruby scoffs. "That guy is the worst."

"The worst," growls Zo.

"It sucks," Ruby adds, "but we've got your back."

"Yeah." Kevin nods so fast his hair becomes a coppery-red blur. "And look at what you've done already. We're making zines and starting a rebellion. We're not just going to let Matt do whatever he likes."

"You're doing the right thing," Jess says with certainty.

"We all are," I say, with a slightly watery smile. "Together."

"And I'm excited about the zine," Zo puts in here. "You're always saying we need to speak up and be heard, but that's not easy for me." We all nod. "The zine will give me a way to say something without having to actually ... *say* something. I'm going to write a poem."

I smile at her. "I guess we should get on with it then," I add, much more cheerfully. "Maybe starting with cutting out some slightly more positive words!"

The others laugh and we get to work, each of us making a double page that will fit together to form our zine.

I'm cutting out a picture of Greta Thunberg and I'm going to draw a speech bubble with a quote of hers on it: *I want you to act as if our house is on fire, because it is.*

"It was a stupid article anyway," Angelika says, as she cuts carefully around a picture of Harry Styles, making sure to keep his luxurious locks intact. "The *Chronicle* is getting worse and worse – like a gossip magazine. I mean, a couple of weeks ago it was hinting there was something going on between you and Aaron!"

"Yeah, imagine," I say weakly over the top of the group's raucous laughter. "What a joke."

"But now Highworth Grange is getting another news source!" Ruby says fiercely. "And this one's actually going to be saying something important."

"I've been thinking though," Jess says with a frown. "How are we going to get the zines to people? Matt's prefects are on every corner. And they'll be watching us especially. There's no way we're going to be able to just hand them out."

"You're right." Kevin grimaces as he continues sketching his Feathers the Pigeon based cartoon. "They'll just find a way to hit us with a load of demerits again."

"Actually," I say slowly, "I had an idea about that . . . but it's SERIOUSLY against the rules."

The others look at me expectantly.

"I know we said we were going to be rebels," I carry on, my words tumbling out quickly, "but I just want to make it clear again that there's NO pressure for anyone to be involved who doesn't want to be. . ."

"Out with it, Effie," Angelika interrupts briskly. "Just tell us what you have in mind."

I hesitate for a second and then I blurt it out. "We're going to break in to the school."

CHAPTER *Twenty-Six*

We're not actually breaking in. We're just not leaving.

After school finishes I head straight for our campaign office. I glance around the corridor to check no one is watching and then slip stealthily inside, closing the door behind me with a soft click.

Now we just have to wait.

The others are already there, and everyone seems in very high spirits. Jess and Zo are our guys "on the outside" in case we need anyone to cover for us. Ruby, Kevin and Angelika are in the office and Ruby is busy admiring Kevin's outfit, which is all black, including a back balaclava that he pulls down to cover the pale moon of his face. I have to admit it is very effective.

"You look like a ninja!" Ruby exclaims.

"I wanted to be prepared," Kevin says modestly. "I brought masks for everyone!" He grins as he hands out the black hats. I look at Angelika and she shrugs, pulling the woollen balaclava over her head. I suppose it does make us look more like rebels. Then Kevin shows us his black utility belt. "It's from an old Batman Halloween costume. I've got all the essentials: torch, tape, snacks, floss. . ."

"Floss?" I say. "What's the floss for?"

"For if we have to, like, hang from the ceiling, *Mission: Impossible* style," Kevin explains patiently.

"But it's just normal floss, right?" I say. "It's not made of very thin titanium or something?"

"Floss is actually very strong," Kevin replies with dignity.

"What snacks have you got?" Ruby asks.

"Percy Pigs."

I turn to Angelika. "Is everything going according to plan?" I ask.

"Yes," she says solemnly, picking up a clipboard off the desk. "We've gone through the checklist several times. We've propped the window open in the girls' toilets by science block . . . just a crack so no one will notice. That's our escape route." She gestures to the map she's drawn on.

I nod. "Good."

"I have to say, Effie," Ruby pipes up from the purple beanbag, "when you said we might have to break a few rules, I didn't realize we were going straight to breaking and entering."

"We're not breaking and entering," I point out, rubbing my clammy hands on the sides of my blazer. "We're just sort of . . . staying and then . . . leaving."

"At least say 'breaking out'," Kevin sighs. "So much cooler."

"Speaking of which," Ruby says, "Kev and I have been working on a theme tune."

"A theme tune?" I wrinkle my nose in confusion.

"You know, like Bond, *Mission: Impossible*. We've got to have a theme tune for our high-stakes caper!"

"Oh, right," I say as Kevin and Ruby start humming and making random "KAPOW" noises which I think are supposed to indicate the moments when the stakes are particularly high.

Eventually they finish and look at Angelika and me expectantly.

"Great," I say.

"Really . . . good," Angelika agrees.

"I think we probably need to start being totally silent now though," I add quickly, before they begin on what they call the "extended remix". "It's probably time for us to move to phase two."

"Alertness level seven." Kevin nods knowingly. "Code name PERCY . . . after the pigs. Everyone synchronize your watches." He presses the screen of his digital watch with a couple of small beeps.

Phase two is not really glamorous enough for it to need a code name. It basically means we lock ourselves in the cupboard, turn the lights off and sit in silence while we wait for everyone to leave. Then we just have to wait for the caretaker to complete his checks.

I don't know if you've ever sat in a dark cupboard with your heart thumping in your chest and three of your best friends trying to be totally silent, but even a few minutes feels like a lifetime. I try not to think about how many school rules we must be breaking at this point. I keep telling myself that because we're not stealing or vandalizing anything it must be fine … but it's hard to believe when I've been an ardent rule follower for my whole entire life.

The only sound is the occasional rustle from Kevin's sweet packet. I can hear the ragged sound of my own breathing as the seconds and the minutes pass. I try to meditate, but my mind is spinning around and around like a Catherine wheel. I can't stop jiggling my legs. As the silence stretches out and out, further and further, I start to think I might burst.

Suddenly, someone jiggles the door handle. The sound of it is like an explosion ripping through the room.

I manage to keep my reaction down to a small high squeak that I hope can't be heard outside.

The four of us remain frozen in the darkness. I'm holding my breath, but as the seconds pass, I realize that the caretaker has obviously moved on. We sit for a few more minutes.

"Do you think he's gone?" Angelika whispers.

BEEP BEEP BEEP BEEP. Kevin's watch alarm

starts going off, pealing through the air.

"Sorrysorrysorry," he mumbles, fighting with the buttons. "I can't see the..."

"Let me get the torch," Angelika whispers, reaching for it. She turns it on and it immediately starts flashing like crazy, like we're at the world's weirdest disco. I realize with a sinking heart that I've picked up my dad's old torch and it's currently flashing SOS around the room while Kevin's alarm continues its shrill wail.

The light goes off abruptly, at the same time as the alarm stops. We are all holding our breath.

"Well," I say, trying to keep the hysteria from bubbling up in my voice. "Let's hope everyone's gone because that wasn't our most stealthy moment."

Moving over to the door, I turn the lock and then I slowly, slooooowly turn the handle, before cautiously pulling the door open a crack. There are no lights on outside. I pause for a second, straining my ears, but I can hear nothing.

With a pounding heart I push the door all the way open and step into the corridor. There's not a sound, and in the darkness, normal, ordinary things like lockers and tables loom as hulking shadows. I stand still for a few more seconds.

"I think the coast is clear." My voice sounds thin and reedy as I call back to the others. They bustle out behind me, turning on their torches, this time without incident.

"Creepy," Ruby says, and her voice echoes a little.

I nod. It is creepy. It's like the school is suddenly a totally different place.

"There aren't any lasers." Kevin sounds disappointed. "I thought there'd be, you know, like a load of red lines all moving about and I'd have to flip and weave in and out of them."

"I don't think the school's security budget is quite up to that," I say.

"I guess I did my mum's yoga-for-beginners DVD for NOTHING." He sighs bitterly. "Although to be fair, most of it was about lying on the floor like a log. Quite relaxing actually."

"So," Angelika cuts in. "Let's get on with it, shall we?"

"Phase three," Ruby confirms.

"Code name SKITTLES," Kevin says, producing a packet from his belt. "This thing's actually great," he says, twisting the belt around. "Maybe I should try and make it a fashion choice. . ."

"Anyway," I interrupt. "Phase three, let's go."

The zines, hundreds of them, are stacked up in the office and we each take a pile. Angelika, Kevin and I slip zines into the rows and rows of lockers, while Ruby shoots them under classroom doors. Ruby and Kevin hum their song and I must admit it all adds to the adrenaline-fuelled sense that we're on a mission of great importance. We work our way towards the canteen, where we leave zines on as many seats as we can before we run out of copies.

"That should get the word out," Angelika says with satisfaction.

"Yeah," I say. "Let's get out ourselves now, shall we?"

As one we turn for the girls' toilets.

"Nice work, team," says Kevin. "Anybody want a Haribo?"

CHAPTER *Twenty-Seven*

OUR FELLOW STUDENTS,

We bring you this zine as a way of spreading our **MESSAGE** to the **WORLD**. The destruction of this planet **IS HAPPENING**. We need to take this disaster seriously.

Time and time again we are told that kids can't change things. Well, we've seen that's not true. We've seen kids protesting, we've seen kids meeting world leaders, and we've seen kids making change happen.

We refuse to stand idly by and do nothing to protect the planet that provides for us **ALL**. There is **NO PLANET B**.

So, what can you do? Well, you can read this zine, which is full of facts (and then pass it on or recycle it, please!). You can raise money to support environmental charities like the ones listed in the back of this zine. Or you can help us make **MORE** zines and share them with your friends. Get creative! Let's get the word out there!

We want to make Highworth Grange a better place, a place that cares about what goes on outside its walls. So we're urging our fellow students to donate towards a local river clean-up taking place next Saturday.

Finally, you can join us in pledging to make Highworth Grange more eco-friendly by writing a letter to the head teacher asking for change, or leaving a suggestion in the school council suggestion box.

Oh, and speaking of the school council ... let's not let people get away with spreading lies and false information because helping the planet is **NOT CONVENIENT** for them. It won't matter if your new blue football uniforms are bringing out the blue in your eyes when you're living in a desolate wasteland, scrounging for biscuit crumbs! Matt Spader has been against the Green Deal from the start. Now he's intending to take advantage of a loophole in the school rules to make himself the permanent president ... even though he was never elected.

If you think this is wrong, then please, make sure you vote against his appointment. The people's voices need to be heard! The vote is next Saturday (yes, the same day as the river clean-up), and, coincidentally, Matt has organized a party that day. No one is saying you have to choose between pizza and democracy – we're just asking you to use your vote first. The polls open at 9:00 a.m.

JOIN OUR REVOLUTION!

THE HIGHWORTH GRANGE
ECO-WARRIORS

A Few Facts About Plastic

- A million plastic bottles are bought around the world every minute.

- Plastic is killing more than 1.1 million seabirds and animals every year.

- There are five trillion pieces of plastic in our oceans. That's enough to circle the Earth over 400 times!!

- The average person eats 70,000 microplastics each year. That's 100 bits in every meal! Gross!!!!

Our Manifesto
HIGHWORTH GRANGE – REDUCE! REUSE! RECYCLE!

A PLAN FOR MAKING OUR SCHOOL GREENER!

1. REDUCE PLASTIC!
Abolish plastic bottles in the canteen and encourage people to bring reusable bottles from home and to fill them at the water fountains. Our aim is to get rid of all single-use plastic in the canteen in the next year.

2. GREEN-FINGERED GARDENERS!
The land behind the science block is the perfect place for a community vegetable patch and a wild flower garden. We'll be collecting and reusing old tins, bottles, trays – anything we can find to plant seeds and plants in. Growing some of our own food cuts back on food miles and plastic waste, and wild flowers attract bees and other insects.

3. RECYCLING BINS!
Raise money to get recycling bins in the canteen and classrooms. Paper, plastic, cardboard, drinks cans – all of these things can be recycled. And start a compost station, so that we can turn food waste into compost for the garden.

An Eco Word Search

E	Z	R	I	P	L	A	S	T	I	C
R	N	S	E	G	H	J	L	W	N	M
U	P	V	K	U	E	G	R	O	W	R
B	W	G	I	Q	S	R	X	R	F	E
B	A	S	W	R	D	E	Z	L	U	D
I	S	O	Y	E	O	E	J	D	Q	U
S	T	P	L	C	Y	N	A	X	G	C
H	E	W	N	Y	K	I	M	U	C	E
D	F	R	J	C	A	W	B	E	E	S
B	O	T	T	L	E	S	M	P	N	A
A	G	Y	D	E	Q	J	F	W	K	T

PLASTIC   GREEN   WORLD
REDUCE   BOTTLES   ENVIRONMENT
REUSE   WASTE   GROW
RECYCLE   BEES   RUBBISH

A POEM

Sometimes I feel small
Almost like I'm not here
At all
But the grass is soft
Under my feet
And the air smells like
freshly sharpened pencils
It reminds me
I am real
I am part of the world
I belong to it
And it belongs to me

CHAPTER *Twenty-Eight*

"Do you think people will have read it yet?" I ask anxiously as Angelika and I make our way to school the next morning.

She laughs. "They won't be there yet, so no. But they'll read it soon, don't worry."

I swallow. "Do you think we're going to get in trouble?"

There's a pause and then Angelika shakes her head. "We didn't even do anything wrong," she says. "Not really."

We near the school gates. My mouth goes suddenly dry as I imagine crime scene tape and detectives with tiny notebooks and forensics teams in white overalls dusting for prints. My heart patters wildly and I feel a little clammy. I just hope Ms Shaarawi doesn't make the whole school do a lie detector test.

But when we reach the main school building, it's a massive anti-climax – everyone is just milling about like normal. Unless there are some undercover agents who make very convincing fourteen-year-old students, it doesn't look like the authorities are involved.

We meet the rest of the group, who are obviously trying their best not to look shifty. Kevin is even whistling a jaunty little tune. To be honest it's making him more conspicuous, but I appreciate the effort.

"Well?" I hiss. "Have you heard anything?"

"Nothing," Ruby says. "And if there was anything to hear, you know I would have heard it."

That's true. Ruby has a spectacular knack of getting gossip first.

"You mean no one's talking about the zine?" I feel like a fast-deflating balloon. "After we practically risked our lives breaking in to the school?"

"Breaking *out*, remember," Kevin points out.

"I don't think we exactly risked our lives," Angelika says.

"But we could have done!" I exclaim, now irrationally angry. "For all we know there could have been red lasers and savage guard dogs and an alarm system with prison bars that slide across the windows!"

"This seems like something we should have discussed *before* we broke out," Ruby murmurs.

"Well, apparently it was for NOTHING." I huff. "We could all be sent to prison and we haven't even made a difference!"

"Effie, you know you asked when you'd ever been dramatic. . ." Ruby smirks.

"Fine," I say after a moment. "Maybe I'm being a tiny bit dramatic. Let's just go in and let events unfold as they may." I stand up straight and shake my hair back. I decide to channel Anne Boleyn, off to her execution. *Dignity*, I tell myself. *Dignity*.

By lunchtime I'm having real trouble with the whole dignity thing.

"No one is saying anything about the zine!" I say as we trudge towards our office. "I haven't heard a peep!"

"To be fair you haven't really talked to anyone except us," Angelika says.

"Yes, but it's not. . ." I wave my hands around. "Out there, in the air, you know. It's not causing a storm. We'd know if it was."

"Maybe it's causing a quiet storm," Kevin says stoutly.

"Like a heavy shower," Jess adds.

"I saw a couple of girls reading it in registration," Zo says mildly.

I whip round. "Did you?" I ask. "Were they saying anything? What did they say?"

"I – I didn't hear anything," Zo manages, looking slightly taken aback by my energy.

I take a deep breath. "Sorry," I say. "I guess I'm still a bit on edge."

We go into our office.

"Maybe we can GET people talking about it," Ruby says thoughtfully. "You know, by casually asking people a few leading questions."

"Like what?" I ask.

"Like, Oh wow, I love your new haircut. Speaking of cuts, have you read that article about how Matt Spader cut the Green Deal? It was in that brilliant new zine."

"That's a pretty impressive segue," I admit.

"Look at this." Kevin stoops to the ground. "It's for you, Effie."

It's a folded-over piece of paper with my name typed on the front.

I open it, and gasp as I scan the words there.

EFFIE,

WANT DIRT ON MATT SPADER?
MEET ME BEHIND THE TREES
BY MUSIC BLOCK AFTER SCHOOL.

A FRIEND

"Someone wants to help us," I say slowly.

"I've got a bad feeling about this," says Kevin. "Who knows if you can trust it."

"Yeah, it could be a trap," Angelika warns. "You know Matt will be angry about the zine."

"It could be a hitman, Effie!" Ruby's eyes gleam with what I think is a little too much excitement.

"That's a risk we're going to have to take," I reply. "If there's something out there that can destroy Matt Spader then we need to find it."

CHAPTER Twenty-Nine

In the end Ruby decides to come with me. "You might need backup," she says.

I am perfectly capable of looking after myself (I do have a brown belt in judo ... which is actually the first belt you get, but still – I look pretty ferocious when I'm wearing it) but I'm glad to have her there.

Especially because this patch of trees by the music block suddenly feels a bit creepy. I guess when you're waiting to meet a mysterious source with shadowy motives who claims they're going to help you to bring down your nemesis, it's not the most typical of situations.

"Well," I say, wrapping my arms around my waist for warmth. "We're here. Where are they?"

"I knew it was a set-up," Ruby says, narrowing her eyes. "From here I can see at least half a dozen potential attack points."

"Attack points?" I say.

"You're in too deep," Ruby says. "This thing probably goes all the way to the top."

"The top of what?" I ask.

Ruby shrugs. "You know, like … the *top*. MI5, CIA, NASA."

"You think NASA are interested in Matt Spader?"

"I've always said there was something off about that boy," Ruby muses. "Maybe he's not … *of this world*."

"I think Matt Spader is a lot of things," I say. "But I don't think he's an actual alien."

"It would be the perfect cover…" Ruby says, almost to herself.

"Wait!" I exclaim. "What's that?" I move further into the trees and there, tied to one of the branches, is another note with my name on it. I read it.

LOOK UNDER THE BENCH IN FRONT OF
THE TREES.

"What is this, an Easter egg hunt?" Ruby huffs. "Someone's wasting our time."

"Maybe not," I say. "Let's go and have a look."

We head back towards the music block and sit on the bench in front of the trees. I run my fingers carefully underneath.

"There's nothing here," I say.

"I knew it," Ruby says.

"Wait!" My fingers hit something. "There *is* something. I think it's taped on." I tug the object and it comes away in my hand.

It's a USB stick.

"Oh my God," Ruby says. "We're like actual spies! I told you this was MI5. What's on it? Encrypted data files? Surveillance footage?"

"I've got a cable in my bag," I gasp, already rummaging around with shaking fingers. "We can plug it into my phone."

We plug the stick into my phone. There's only one file on it. An audio file. I look at Ruby and she nods. I hit play.

"They're all idiots, of course," Matt's voice booms from my speaker, and I let out a squeak and quickly turn it down, glancing around to make sure we're still alone. "I can't believe how easy it is really. All

I had to do was suck up to Mr Jameson a bit, laugh at his stupid jokes, and flirt with Catriona – let her think she had a chance. Now no one's going to listen to anything Effie says. I've had enough of her and her stupid friends getting in my way. She's such a loud, bossy. . ."

Here the recording is muffled – I think there's someone else talking to him. Then Matt's voice comes back loud and clear.

"I'm not worried about that. The rest of the students are totally clueless. I wave a piece of pizza in front of their dumb faces and they'll follow me anywhere. Morons. Don't get me wrong. I love Aaron, you know I do, but he's so soft. Being on the school council used to mean something. Now he's afraid to use the council to get stuff done. Ever since he started hanging out with that girl, he's changed. I'm not a bad guy, I'm just not going to put my life on hold for a few plastic bottles, you know?"

There's another muffled comment then. It's impossible to recognize the voice.

"Who cares about being fair!" Matt's laughter fills the air. "My dad always says, you've got to look after yourself first. I'm obviously the best choice for the school, but I can't rely on these dummies to realize it.

By making sure the vote doesn't happen I'm actually looking after everyone. You understand, don't you?"

With a click the recording ends.

We sit in silence. "Wow," Ruby says finally.

"Yeah," I croak.

"I mean . . . wow." She shakes her head. "This is it, you know." A slow smile spreads across Ruby's face. "You've got him. You play this for the school and NO ONE is going to support him any more. He's on tape calling them all idiots!"

"Yeah." I nod. "This could be the end of him. . ." I take a deep breath. "If we use it."

CHAPTER *Thirty*

"What do you mean *if* we use it?" Kevin says.

"Sssshhhh!" I hiss, looking around the crowded canteen. "This is sensitive information."

"We know it's sensitive information," Kevin says in a whisper that's not exactly subtle. "That's why you've got to use it! It will finish him off."

"But it's sneaky," I say. "He obviously didn't know he was being recorded. People have a right to privacy. There are principles at stake!"

"The school has the right to know that this is what he thinks of them," Ruby argues.

"Maybe." I frown. "It's not like the recording is proof of him doing anything *wrong* … apart from being a huge jerk, I mean. And what about Catriona and Aaron – it might hurt them if the recording comes out too."

"Catriona hasn't exactly been a friend to you, Effie," Jess points out.

"I know, but ... I don't want to sink to Matt's level." I look over at Angelika. "You've been quiet," I say. "What do you think?"

She stays silent for a moment, her head slightly bowed in thought. "I think you're right," she says finally. "Releasing the recording is something Matt would do without a second thought. He obviously thought he was having a private conversation. None of us would want everyone to hear everything we say. If we're not trying to do better than him then what's the point of opposing him?"

"I agree," Zo says quietly.

"I can't believe this!" Ruby exclaims. "Someone took a risk making that recording for us and we're not even going to use it."

I nod, and a smile spreads over my face. "Isn't that great?" I say. "There's someone else on our side. Someone who actually knows Matt. Someone sticking up for us." The thought of it is like a warm chocolate chip cookie. "Maybe, just maybe, people are starting to listen to us."

"Uh-oh," Kevin mutters, looking over my shoulder. "Incoming."

I turn around to see Matt bearing down on us. He doesn't look happy.

"What *is* this?" His voice is loud as he slams a copy of the zine on the table.

"I believe they're called *zines*," I say politely.

"*You* did this," he hisses, pointing at me.

"I actually think it was the Highworth Grange Eco-Warriors," Angelika says, leafing through the zine.

"They seem cool," Ruby says.

"Well, they've done it all for nothing, whoever they are," Matt sneers. "No one's reading it. My prefects have been collecting loads of copies and putting them where they belong. In the bin." There is a short, simmering silence. "I just wonder how you managed to hand them all out. I'd hate to think you broke any school rules spreading these lies. . ."

"Lies? Is there anything in there that isn't true?" I wait. "Didn't think so. Now if you don't mind, my friends and I would like to get back to our lunch."

Matt's jaw clenches. "You'll be sorry," he snarls before turning and walking away.

"Are you *sure* you don't want to use that recording?"

Ruby sighs, watching Matt's sulky progress out of the canteen.

"He's scared," I say. "We must be doing something right."

Zo nudges my elbow.

"Look," she says, nodding to a girl at the table next to us.

I look over and a little shiver of surprise weasels through me. The girl is wearing a badge pinned to the lapel of her blazer, and – unless my eyes need testing again, which I'm sure they don't because I'm very vigilant about staying up to date on my optician appointments – the badge is the Highworth Grange Eco-Warriors logo from the zine, the letter R made of twigs on top of a leaf.

"That's the third kid I've seen wearing one of those badges," says Zo.

"When did you make badges?" I ask Kevin.

"I didn't." Kevin's eyes are wide. "I have no idea where that's come from."

We all stare at each other. "You mean . . . someone else made them?" Angelika says slowly.

"There's another thing as well," Ruby says. "I heard that Ms Shaarawi is getting the water fountains fixed – I think it was because some students had mentioned it to her."

"It might be nothing," I say.

"Or it might be something," says Angelika.

She's right, I think. Maybe, just maybe, people are starting to listen. . .

CHAPTER *Thirty-One*

The Highworth Grange Chronicle   Issue No. 219   6 April

LOVESTRUCK TEEN
CAUSES EMBARRASSING
SCENES!

By Catriona McGiddens

News in that Highworth Grange Student Council has been rocked by yet more **TURMOIL**, with its president becoming the subject of a vicious smear campaign.

President Matt Spader agreed to sit down with us for an EXCLUSIVE chat.

"I felt it was time to address these problems," Matt says, his brow crinkling in a way that is both thoughtful and presidential. "The last thing I want is more upheaval for the school." The light glints off his golden hair as he bows his

THIS REPORTER'S SPIDEY-SENSES ARE TINGLING. IS THIS THE ONLY REASON FOR THIS GIRL'S CAMPAIGN OF LIES??

head. "I'm not going to name names, because I don't want to be *that* guy, but there's a certain big-haired troublemaker in the school who's trying to stir up drama and turn people against me." Matt shakes his head. "Aaron warned me about her. He said she wants her own way at any cost. He advised me just to ignore her. I tried. But she spread lies about me around the school. It's hard not to take that personally. Someone like that does not have the best interests of the school at heart."

When asked about the motivation of this unnamed person, Matt sighs. "Everyone knows why she's out to get me – it's because she lost the election. Now she wants to undermine the

DEMOCRATIC RESULT. It's my job as president to make sure people get what they voted for."

This reporter's Spidey-senses are **TINGLING**. Is this the **ONLY** reason for this girl's **CAMPAIGN OF LIES??**

Matt squirms in his seat, clearly torn between sharing the truth and compromising the reputation of another student, but I am like a **BLOODHOUND** on the scent of a story and refuse to be deterred.

"There is one other thing," Matt admits finally. "The girl in question has a bit of a crush on me and when I turned her down, well – she was pretty devastated. She started following me around and sending me messages. It was embarrassing." He turns blue eyes on me. "Don't judge her too harshly," he says. "The poor girl is understandably taking it hard."

So there you have it, readers. A **THWARTED ROMANCE** has led to division in our school, and it is up to us to separate the **LIES** from the **TRUTH**. **More on this story as it unfolds...**

CHAPTER *Thirty-Two*

"That . . . that TOAD!" Angelika hisses.

"That is an insult to toads," Ruby joins in, furiously.

"Yeah," Kevin adds, attacking his sketchbook with angry strokes of his pencil. "Don't abuse toads like that. There's nothing as low as Matt Spader. He's the ultimate baddie."

"I can't believe he did this," I say again. My brain is struggling to process the words that are printed in black and white. "All this stuff about me having a crush on him and following him around. None of that happened. No one believes this, do they?" I ask, looking around at them.

There's a brief silence and then everyone starts talking at once, too bright, too hasty.

"No, no!" Angelika insists.

"No one who matters," Kevin says staunchly.

"Jess?" I say, because I can always rely on Jess to tell me the whole truth.

"People are talking about it," she says. "Some people believe it. I keep telling them it's rubbish." Her voice gets quite fierce at the end.

"Yeah, and anyone spreading these stupid rumours will have me to deal with." Ruby smiles a dangerous smile.

Zo grips my clammy hand with hers and squeezes. Even though I'm surrounded by my friends and they're saying all the right things, I still feel sick. Matt might not have used my name but he made it pretty obvious who he was talking about, and now these lies are all over the school. I feel a bit dizzy as I think about walking down the corridors while people whisper about me. I might not be a shrinking violet, but that doesn't mean I want to be in the middle of a load of stupid gossip.

"Do you think Aaron really warned Matt about me?" I ask, my eyes scanning the page.

"I'm sure that's just Matt stirring things up," Angelika says calmly.

"Maybe," I say. "Or maybe Matt's been telling

Aaron some twisted version of events. Of course he's going to believe what his best friend tells him." I sigh. "At this rate even if we DO manage to get Matt out, Aaron will hate me too." I groan. "I thought the problem was not being heard. Now people won't believe me when I do talk."

"Matt doesn't seem to have that problem," Ruby points out. "Even though he's the biggest liar of all."

"It's sexist is what it is," Angelika growls. "Girls have to work so much harder to get people to listen to them."

"Effie, you HAVE to use the recording against him now," Kevin says. "He can't get away with this!"

I think about this for a moment, turning the problem over in my mind.

"No," I say slowly. "I think it's even more important now that we don't. There's nothing on that tape we can argue the people need to know – it's just him being obnoxious. Look at the levels he's stooping to. Lying, manipulating the media... We shouldn't be trying to beat him by playing his game. It's all wrong, what he's doing, and I don't want to be part of it. People will see the truth about him in the end," I add. "He's not *that* good an actor."

"What if he *is* that good?" Jess asks. "What if he

fools them all and cheats his way into the presidency? What if we lose?"

"Then we lose doing the right thing," I say with more certainty than I feel. I know that keeping the recording to ourselves is the right thing to do – but what if it means that the school ends up with someone in charge who doesn't have their best interests at heart, who could actually do harm? Things have got so complicated, and I'm not completely sure what's right and what's wrong any more.

"We keep going," I say. "That's all we *can* do. As Michelle Obama says, *When they go low, we go high.*" And if there's anyone left we can put our trust in now, I think, it must be Michelle.

CHAPTER *Thirty-Three*

STUDENT POLL REVEALS MATT SPADER FIRM FAVE FOR PRESIDENT!

I look at the headline with a sinking heart. The vote is two days away and it's looking like all our hard work might be for nothing.

Not for nothing, I tell myself firmly as I walk home from school. People are starting to respond to our eco-message. I've seen a few more kids wearing badges, and our donation box for the river clean-up was surprisingly full – enough for us to hire a minibus to take us from the school, as well as buy litter pickers and bin bags and gloves. I'm not sure who will actually turn up for the clear-up given it's the same day as Matt's pizza party, but even if it's just us at least we can make a dent in the damage. It feels good to be doing something, even when things feel so hopeless.

My phone beeps in my pocket and I pull it out to look at the message. To my surprise, I see Aaron's name pop up.

DAD FINALLY LETTING ME HAVE
VISITORS. CAN YOU COME OVER?
IT'S IMPORTANT. A

My heart sinks. Whatever Matt's been telling Aaron, it obviously hasn't been good.

Still, I should try and explain my side. I tap out a quick reply saying I'll be over soon and then I head home to change out of my uniform.

It seems like maybe it's polite to bring a gift when arriving with a potential diplomatic crisis. In the end I decide to take a box of chocolates.

Aaron's house is in a really nice part of town. The road is wide and leafy and the house is big and modern with lots of tall glass windows.

I feel a wave of nerves as I knock on Aaron's door. There's something a bit intimidating about all the sharp corners. The nervous feeling intensifies. What am I doing here? The last thing I need is another boy saying he doesn't believe me.

Just then, the door swings open and there's a girl looking up at me. She's about the same age as Lil, with blonde curly hair and big soft brown eyes. She's like the human equivalent of a Labrador puppy, and very cute.

"What's the password?" she asks in a firm voice.

"The password?" I repeat blankly.

The girl folds her arms and looks at me. "Yes. The password."

"Um, can I have a clue?" I ask.

"This is Gryffindor Tower," she says.

"Oh, but then the password is always changing." I frown. "I suppose I could try some of the old ones . . . um, flibbertigibbet? Tapeworm? Banana fritters?"

"It *is* banana fritters!" The little girl looks pleased. "And I like your scarf. I'm Gryffindor too, you know. Because I'm very, very brave."

"Nice," I say. "My sister, Lil, is a full-on Slytherin. I think she's about your age, I don't know if you go to the same school."

"Lil Kostas?" The girl's eyes widen. "*You're* Lil's

sister?" It's like I've just announced I'm related to Harry Potter himself.

A woman appears suddenly behind the girl. "Who is it, Lexie?" she asks. "You know you're not supposed to answer the door." She smiles at me, and I notice she has a little beauty mark above her mouth, just like Aaron. She must be his mum; they look very alike.

"I'm Effie," I say. "I'm a . . . um . . . friend of Aaron's. He asked me over. I bought him these." I clutch the box of Milk Tray like a talisman.

"Oh, how nice!" Aaron's mum says. "He'll be so happy to see you. I think he's going out of his mind with the boredom. His dad's been a bit of a dragon about keeping people away, wouldn't even let him have his phone. . ." She opens the door wider to let me in. "Aaron!" she calls. "There's someone here to see you!" Then she smacks her hand to her forehead with a grimace. "Why am I calling the poor boy when he can't move?!" she says, shaking her head. "Honestly, I'm so scattered what with him being in this accident and his dad being away. Lexie will show you the way, won't you?"

Lexie nods, looking up at me with those big brown eyes, and she takes my hand in hers.

"Come on," she says, "he's in the den." We walk

down a long white corridor. I start to feel like we're on a spaceship or something. This house is even bigger inside than it looked from the street. We walk through an enormous kitchen which is gleaming white with one of those huge space fridges that make all different shaped ice cubes when you press a button.

"Through here," Lexie says, opening a door. "Aaron, your friend is here," she calls. "And she's Lil Kostas's sister!" With that Lexie whisks herself away.

I make my way cautiously through the door. Propped up on the long, squashy, L-shaped sofa with his whole leg in a bright blue cast is Aaron, a PlayStation controller in his hand and a big TV screen showing some kind of racing car game up on the wall.

"Hi, Effie," says Aaron. "Thanks for coming."

"No worries," I say awkwardly. "I brought you these." I hold out the box of chocolates, which is now a bit battered because of how hard I've been clutching it.

"Oh." Aaron's voice is surprised. "Thanks."

There's an awkward silence, and then Aaron clears his throat. "I'd come and say hi, but I'm a bit stuck at the moment." He gestures towards his leg and gives his little half grin.

I walk over and hand him the chocolates.

"This was really nice of you, Kostas," Aaron says, pulling the lid open. He pauses. "Um, quite a few of these are missing."

I peer at the box. "Oh no," I groan. "I knew I should have hidden them inside the vegetable drawer... I put them inside the bran flakes box but Lil must have found them."

Aaron grins. "She's left us the toffees though," he says, taking one and offering the box to me.

"Big of her," I mutter, thinking that we're going to be having a serious talk when I get home.

"Anyway," I say, still standing. "Why did you want to see me?"

He flushes a little. "I wanted to talk to you about something." He gestures to the sofa. "Can you sit down? You're making me feel a bit nervous."

We both laugh then, and there's a bit less awkwardness. I sit down.

"So, it's about the Green Deal," Aaron says, reaching down beside him to pick up a binder. "I'm sure you're doing a great job, but I thought ... well, I've had a few more ideas that I wanted to talk over with you."

In a daze I take the binder he is holding out

and leaf through it. It's a thing of beauty. There is a colour-coded index.

"You made this?" I ask slowly. "Why?"

"In case you haven't noticed, I've got a lot of free time on my hands just sitting around." He taps his leg ruefully. "I've even asked if I can have extra homework, but the teachers can't keep up with me."

I stare at him. He doesn't know, I realize. He doesn't know that the Green Deal has been scrapped. But why hasn't Matt told him? And wouldn't he have read all about it in the *Chronicle*?

"You haven't seen the school paper?" I ask carefully.

Aaron's frown deepens. "No," he says. "There hasn't been another bird in the science block again, has there? Poor old Feathers," he sighs. "Though the memorial service was a nice touch."

"Yeah," I agree, my brain still scrambling to work out what's going on. "And that song Kevin wrote. . ."

"To some you're just a pigeonnnn," Aaron sings a little off-key.

"But you flapped your way into our heartssssss," I join in, momentarily distracted, and we both giggle.

"Anyway," I say, remembering the matter at hand. "It's nothing like that." I hesitate for a second and then reach for my bag with a sigh, pulling out the crumpled newspaper. Angelika says I shouldn't torture myself carrying it around with me, but I actually find that the rage it inspires FUELS me to do better. I hand it over to Aaron without a word.

I watch as he reads it. The frown is back and it gets more and more intense as he gets further on. By the time he drops the newspaper on to his lap his face looks pretty angry.

I swallow. I knew he'd be furious.

"Effie," he begins, his voice hard. "I can't believe this."

"I know how it looks," I start, in a small voice. "I'm so sorry."

"Whhaaaaaaa?" The noise that comes out of me at this point is not very dignified, but Aaron's not paying attention. He's looking at the paper as if it's giving off an offensive smell.

"I can't believe Matt would say all this. I'm really, really sorry." He lifts his eyes to mine. "Are you OK?"

I'm still goggling at him, my mouth slightly open. "You . . . you don't believe him?" I ask.

Aaron huffs. "I think I know you a bit better than that, Effie," he says. "If someone says you don't care about the well-being of the school then they're either stupid or lying. Or both. Don't tell me anyone else believed this?"

"A few people," I say. "I think."

Aaron's brow crumples. "Why would Matt do this in the first place?" he asks. "Did you two have a fight?"

"Yeah," I admit. "After he took over the fete and trashed the Green Deal he's been pretty keen to shut me up."

There's a silence. "Effie, what are you talking about?" Aaron says at last.

"Wait." I stare at him. "You haven't spoken to Matt?"

"Not since the accident," Aaron says. "My dad can be pretty strict. No visitors at all... I wasn't even allowed to have my phone..." He looks at me, and breaks off when he sees my face. "What is it?"

I take a deep breath. Then, as quickly as possible, I outline what's happened while Aaron's been away.

Aaron's mouth drops open a bit more with each sentence. "I had no idea," he says finally. "I asked my dad to at least get an update from Matt on football and council news and he just said everything was fine."

"Everything is definitely NOT fine."

"I can see that."

We both lapse into silence for a moment.

"I never thought I'd be longing for the day when YOU were student council president," I say finally.

Aaron gives a snort of laughter, but then he sighs.

"I can't believe this," he says. "I broke my leg, they can't just give my presidency away."

"They can, Aaron," I say gently. Aaron's not used to things working against him. "It's the rules. Trust me, I checked."

"But Matt's supposed to be my best friend." There's a genuine thread of pain in Aaron's words. "How was he going to explain any of this to me?"

"He'd probably tell you he was forced into it," I sigh. "Or that it was my fault somehow."

"Sorry, Effie," Aaron says glumly, slumping further into his seat. "Just when I thought that being stuck here couldn't get any worse."

I look at him, stuck with his leg out in front of him, still a little pale and sad looking, and I feel another rush of anger towards Matt. I think about what he says on that horrible recording, and how lucky I am to have my friends. It's just another reason I can't let Matt win.

"Well, don't give up just yet," I say firmly. "I'm going to do everything I can to stop him. If I have my way, you'll keep your presidency."

There's a ghost of a smile on his face. "Thanks, Effie," Aaron says. "You're my knight in shining armour."

"Well, someone has to be." I take another toffee from the chocolate box. "Just remember that when we're talking about my future policy ideas."

CHAPTER *Thirty-Four*

It's all very well telling Aaron I'm going to save his presidency, but the next day I'm feeling a lot less positive. Tomorrow is the first day of the holidays and the vote – and this is feeling a bit too familiar.

I've been here before, the day before the big election, and it didn't exactly end well. The familiar feeling of butterflies in my stomach, the burden of responsibility, the sense that people are counting on me and I might let them down ... it's a lot to handle. Even for someone who wants to run a whole country one day.

Somehow I make it through the morning's lessons. At lunch, I head to the canteen, my head spinning round and round. One minute I convince myself everything will be OK, but then the doubt starts creeping in again. It's like being on a constant merry-go-round. Not a fun one with beautiful horses called ROSALIND, more like a terrible one full of anxiety and Matt's self-satisfied grin swirling round and round like some scary clown-mask-based nightmare.

"Effie, there you are!" Angelika rushes up to me. "I've just seen two more people wearing the badges!"

"The eco-warriors badges?"

She nods. "I'm telling you, Effie, people are responding to the zine! It's getting through to them. I overheard someone talking about the vote tomorrow. And yesterday there was a line of people with reusable bottles at the water fountain!"

Angelika's words lift my heart. Is it really possible that things are going to change?

"I just wish we had more time," I say. "Have we done enough? Is there any chance we can beat him?"

"There's always a chance," Angelika says firmly.

"Wrong, as usual," an unwelcome voice interrupts.

I spin around on my heel and find myself face-to-face with Matt. These showdowns are getting to be something of a habit, and one that I could definitely live without.

He stands there with his bag slung over his

shoulder looking completely relaxed, an easy smile on his face. I know that I – on the other hand – look like a girl who hasn't been sleeping very well, whose enormous curly hair is growing wilder by the minute.

"There *is* always a chance," I say. I'm proud that my voice doesn't waver.

Matt shrugs. "You keep telling yourself that," he says.

He looks like someone who's already won. I know in that second that the efforts I've made haven't been enough, that the zines haven't been enough. Maybe if we'd had more time. Maybe if we released the recording of him. But I don't want that. I don't want him to change us – to make our behaviour worse to match his.

He's made fun of me, he's lied about me, he's silenced me.

He's done all those things and he's still going to win. There are no consequences, not for him.

Before I even know what I'm doing, I pull a chair out, and its legs scrape along the canteen floor with an audible screech. I climb on to the chair. Then I climb on to the table.

The canteen is busy, full of students getting lunch and chatting and laughing, and now they're all turning to look at me. The room falls silent.

I look down at Angelika and her eyes are round, full of questions. *What are you doing?*

What *am* I doing?

"Hello," I say awkwardly. My voice is a little bit squeaky.

I clear my throat. All the eyes burn into me.

"What's she doing?" I hear Ruby hiss.

I stand up straighter, hold my head high. "Hello," I say again, my voice steadier this time. "For those of you who don't know, I'm Effie Kostas. I need to tell you all something important."

"Let us eat!" a voice calls from the back. A few people snigger.

I force a smile. "You can eat and listen," I say. I take a deep breath. "Matt Spader is trying to cheat his way into the student council presidency." A little murmur of unease goes around the room.

"I'm not saying that because I don't like him. It's a fact. He's found an old loophole in the school rules that means if you don't come out and vote against him tomorrow, he'll be president instead of Aaron." I look down at Matt, who is still smiling in an amused sort of way.

"Matt is counting on all of you not to turn up

tomorrow. That's why he's organized a party on the same day. He's hoping you'll think it's not important. But it *is* important, and here's why: instead of raising money to help the school become more green, Matt wants to buy new football uniforms for himself and his mates on the team. Instead of letting the council choose prefects to represent them, he's cheated the system and appointed his mates. They can hand out demerits and punishments to anyone he doesn't like. He's lied to the school paper. He said that Aaron knew what was going on – that's not true. I saw Aaron yesterday, and he didn't know about ANY of this. Matt has manipulated everyone to get his own way. If he wins tomorrow, he'll be president for good. A president that no one voted for.

"Now I know that Matt has tried to make me out to be a sore loser, a stalker, a loud, bossy troublemaker. It's easy to do that because I'm a girl. If I stand up for myself then he can just point to that as more evidence. Well, I've had enough. I'm telling you the truth, and you can decide whether you're going to listen to it or not. Whether you're going to do anything about it or not.

"There's one last thing." I take a deep breath. "You've all seen the zines around school. Well, I was the one who broke into the school and put them in people's lockers. I know I could get in trouble for that but I want you to know it was me. You deserve the truth. Please come and vote tomorrow. Don't let anyone trick you out of having a voice." I stop then, the silence in the canteen spreading out, thick like butter on bread. "That's it," I say finally. "That's what I wanted to say."

With all the dignity I can muster I climb down from the table.

The silence continues for a long painful moment before it's broken by a sharp voice

"Effie Kostas!" I wheel around to find Miss Sardana standing by the canteen door. She points at me. "Head teacher's office. Now."

CHAPTER *Thirty-Five*

Miss Sardana and I walk through the corridor in tense silence.

"You're back then," I say finally, unable to bear it any more.

"I got back yesterday. It seems you've been rather busy." Miss Sardana's voice is dry.

"Yes," I say, "there's been a lot going on." Now that the adrenaline is leaving my body I feel strangely close to tears. "I wish you'd been here, miss," I add.

Miss Sardana shoots me a look that I can't quite read before knocking on Ms Shaarawi's door.

"Come in," comes the crisp call from within.

"Wait here," Miss Sardana says to me. "Ms

Shaarawi needs to hear about your behaviour. We'll call you in in a minute."

A couple of minutes later, Miss Sardana opens the door wide and gestures for me to come in.

For the second time in the last couple of weeks I find myself in the head teacher's office. Unfortunately, this time Yia-yia's not here to whisk me away.

Ms Shaarawi is leaning back against the desk her arms folded, and a frown on her face.

"Effie," she says, "please take a seat."

I sit down, folding my hands in my lap, and staring down at my interlocked fingers.

"Effie," she says. "You are one of our best and brightest pupils. You've got an exemplary record, not so much as a demerit on your file, nothing but glowing reports from your teachers. And yet in the past few weeks, I'm hearing reports of behavioural issues, outbursts, detention, and now, this disruption in the canteen." She gives me a long and searching look. "What on earth is going on?" she asks.

"It's a long story," I say.

"Well, there's plenty of time," Ms Shaarawi says. "We want to help, Effie. Why don't you just tell us what happened."

And so I do. I tell them about the student council

meeting where Matt scrapped the Green Deal. I tell them about getting detention. About the school paper making things up. I leave out some parts, like breaking into the school – I feel sure Miss Sardana must have heard that bit of my speech but she doesn't mention it. I wouldn't mind so much if it had just been me, but they could tear out my fingernails one by one and I would never, NEVER reveal the names of my comrades.

I talk and talk and talk for ages, and they don't interrupt me. They just listen.

When I finish my story I see Ms Shaarawi and Miss Sardana share a look, but I'm not quite sure what it means. Sometimes I think grown-ups have their own code that kids haven't quite learned yet. Still, I suppose that's fair. They don't get us sometimes either.

"Effie, why didn't you come to me with any of this sooner?" Ms Shaarawi asks finally.

"You, miss?" I frown. "I don't know. I didn't think the head teacher would care that much. At first it was a small problem and then . . . I didn't know if you'd believe me. Mr Jameson didn't."

"Mr Jameson is a new teacher," Miss Sardana says. "He doesn't know you as well as we do. He doesn't have access to the information that Ms Shaarawi has."

"I – I suppose," I say.

"And of course I care about these things, Effie," Ms Shaarawi says gently. "I'm the head teacher. That means that the well-being of my students is the most important thing to me."

We sit quietly for a moment.

"Well," Ms Shaarawi says finally. "Given the circumstances, I don't think any further action is needed with regards to your behaviour, Effie, but I hope that next time you have a problem you will come to me or Miss Sardana." She looks at her watch. "There's very little of the day left now. You'd better head home."

"Oh," I say. Being sent home feels almost as bad as detention.

"It's not a punishment, Effie. We're in last period now anyway. Best to let everyone calm down, I think."

I nod. "Thanks, miss," I say. I gather up my things to leave.

Miss Sardana takes me out into the hall. "Did you tell her about me breaking into school?" I ask.

"No, I didn't." A smile tugs at the corner of her mouth. "I saw your zine, Effie. I thought it was excellent."

"Really?" I ask.

Miss Sardana looks round quickly. She grabs the lapel on her jacket and twists it round. And there, pinned to the back, is a Highworth Grange Eco-Warriors pin.

CHAPTER *Thirty-Six*

The morning of the vote dawns bright and sunny. It's lovely, optimistic weather, but I feel anxious and full of nervous flutterings.

My phone beeps. Our group chat has been going wild all morning. I'm surprised the sheer number of *Hamilton* GIFs Angelika has sent isn't causing my phone to melt down.

As much as my friends' support warms my heart (and it truly does), I already knew I could count on them to turn up today. What if no one else comes to vote? What if it's just the six of us? It's going to give Matt even more ammunition to make me out to be a laughing stock once this is all over.

Plus, it's the river clean-up later. I haven't managed

to get anyone to sign up. There's going to be a minibus turning up and just the six of us getting on it.

I look at myself in the mirror. A panicked girl in purple pyjamas stares back at me. My hair is even wilder than usual and I attempt to smooth the curls a little while having a stern word with myself. What would Malala say? I ask myself. She'd ask me if I should care about looking foolish when I'm standing up for what I know is right.

"NO I SHOULD NOT," I yell aloud.

"Who are you talking to?" Lil's voice comes from behind me and I jump.

"No one," I say quickly.

"It was Malala again, wasn't it?" Lil looks at me pityingly.

"What are you doing here?" I ask.

"Came to give you this." Lil holds out a purple glittery scrunchie. "I know it wasn't the best luck last time, but THIS time I know it will work." I take the scrunchie, the same one Lil gave me the day I lost the election to Aaron, between my fingers.

"OK," I say, pulling my hair up into a ponytail. "Time to change our luck, scrunchie. Time to make stuff happen."

"First imaginary Malala, now a scrunchie," Lil

sighs. "We need to get you some more friends."

"I have friends!" I exclaim.

"Well, why don't you talk to one of them then?" Before I can come up with a snappy comeback, Lil turns and sashays out the door. "Also," she calls over her shoulder, "Dad says to tell you it's almost time to go."

I glance at the clock. She's right, I need to get a move on. I pull on a pair of jeans and a stripy long-sleeved top, then put on the T-shirt Ruby made for me. It's white and it says ECO-WARRIOR on the front and BIG HAIR SHOWS SHE CARES on the back, underneath my name.

On my desk is a megaphone I borrowed off Iris and I take that too.

"Do you really think the megaphone is necessary?" Dad eyes it uneasily as I appear in the kitchen. "You don't usually have much trouble making yourself heard."

"What if there's a crowd and they are riled up, Dad?" I ask, pinching a piece of toast from the pile Mum is making and spreading it thickly with Nutella. "What if they need direction or an inspiring speech and they can't hear me over the sound of their protest songs?"

"I hope you're managing your expectations,

Effitsa," Dad says, blowing on his cup of tea. "Don't forget you've not had long to organize this."

"People will come," I say. It sounds suspiciously as though I'm trying to convince myself.

"We just don't want you to be disappointed," Mum adds.

"Effie has it all under control." Yia-yia comes sweeping in, wearing a floral kimono, a mask of light pink cream spread across her face. "She is a Kostas. She has the spirit of our ancestors running through her veins."

"Yia-yia says we were practically born on Mount Olympus." Lil hops up on to the counter, her legs swinging as she dips a spoon in the Nutella jar. "It makes total sense to me. I always identified with Zeus. Just need to get my hands on a few of those lightning bolts."

"Well, terrifying as that sounds, let's drop your sister off at the school, shall we?" Dad turns to me. "We'll meet you at the river once we get back from Lil's judo class."

"Even Yia-yia?" I say, and everyone giggles because the thought of the most glamorous woman on earth trudging through the mud to clean a river is a funny one.

Yia-yia raises an eyebrow. "I shall be supervising,"

she says regally. "What is the dress code for the event?"

"I have some old jeans you can borrow upstairs," Mum says.

"Jeans?" Yia-yia wrinkles her nose. "I am not a cowgirl."

"OK," Mum says. "Well, I'm sure anything will do. Now let's get moving please, everyone in the car, go, go, go."

"I think I'll walk actually," I say. "It will give me time to think."

I cut through on the footpath, little puffs of my breath showing slightly in the still chilly air. In the end I arrive at the school a few minutes after 9:00 a.m. I'm the only one there and I stand in the quiet.

It's a bit strange that *no one's* here. Not even my friends. I thought they'd be here by now.

I decide I might as well go in and vote. There's a table set up just inside the door and a very weary-looking teacher is sitting there with a big pile of marking.

"Take a ballot and fill it out." He gestures to the table. "Then drop it into the box."

I take the piece of paper and read it.

EMERGENCY MOTION TO MAKE MATT SPADER JUNIOR STUDENT COUNCIL PRESIDENT. ARE YOU IN FAVOUR?

I put my big cross carefully next to the NO, and fold the piece of paper in half, dropping it in the box. My single piece of paper falling in that totally empty box sounds like a great echoing crash.

I go back outside. No one is here. *It's still early,* I think. It's still early. The time ticks on, great, gaping moments of nothing.

No one's coming

No one's coming

No one's coming.

CHAPTER *Thirty-Seven*

"Effie!"

I swivel round and there's Angelika, Ruby, Kevin, Jess and Zo.

"You're here!" I exclaim. They've never looked better. All of them are wearing the T-shirts that we made for this event, but they're also carrying signs.

"What's this?" I ask, taking the sign Angelika hands me. It has all sorts of animals around the words:

OUR PLANET
OUR HOME

Zo's says: WHAT WOULD DAVID DO? And it has a picture of David Attenborough in a red sparkly heart.

"Let me glitter you!" Ruby rushes forward, and I notice that the others all have green glitter on their faces. "Don't worry," she adds with a grin. "It's eco-glitter, biodegradable. Quick, before everyone else gets here."

"Thanks," I say, allowing Ruby to sweep the glitter in big streaks across my cheeks. "But I think it's just going to be us."

"Effie, you dummy," Ruby says, pausing in her glittering for a second. "Where do you think we've been? There's a lorry broken down in the road back there, we've been sitting behind it for HOURS. . ."

"About thirty minutes," Angelika puts in.

"It's moved now," Kevin says eagerly, brandishing his banner. "And they're all on their way."

"Who are?" I frown. "And what's with these signs? Someone please explain!"

"It was your speech yesterday," Angelika says.

"It DEFINITELY got people talking," Ruby adds.

"They were all asking us about the eco-warriors," Jess explains. "They had no idea Matt was up to no good."

"People *love* the zine, Effie!" Kevin eyes are shining. "All those badges we kept seeing – there's like an underground fan club."

"Really?" I ask, dazed.

They all nod. "So we thought we'd organize something for you," Angelika says. "As a surprise. . ."

Angelika's interrupted as the cars arrive. Lots of them. There are kids piling out of cars, arriving on scooters and bikes. They're wearing eco-warrior badges and clutching signs and banners. Shouting and laughing. Another big group show up on foot.

All of the signs they start waving have slogans on them like:

SUPPORT THE GREEN DEAL!

I'M A HIGHWORTH GRANGE ECO-WARRIOR!

I even see one that says I'M WITH HER and then underneath is a picture of a girl with truly enormous hair.

"Oh!" I gasp, my knees feeling suddenly weak. Relief and nerves are all muddled up together inside me. "People are coming. They listened to us!"

"Yes they did!" Angelika says. "So you'd better dust off that megaphone."

With that the gang starts to spread out, directing

people in towards the vote. There's a steady stream of people going in and coming out, laughing and joking and high-fiving each other.

After they come out, Ruby and Kevin start rounding them up into a big crowd outside the school gates. Even Zo is helping. I feel like the Grinch with my heart growing three sizes in my chest.

"Almost the whole school is here!" Jess murmurs next to me, awe in her voice.

We've won, I realize. There's no way Matt's going to be president. Not with all this lot turning out to vote against him.

"Hello, Effie." I turn and see Miss Sardana standing behind me.

"Hello, miss," I say, dazed. "What are you doing here?"

"I'm here for the river clean-up, of course," Miss Sardana says.

That's when I realize it's not just students who are here. There are parents and grandparents and brothers and sisters. All sorts of people coming together to make a difference.

"They didn't just come to vote today, Effie," Angelika appears at my side. "That's what I was trying to tell you. They're here for the clean-up."

"What . . . all of them?" I ask.

They both nod.

"I think we're going to need a bigger bus." I swallow as I look at all the people milling around in front of me.

Miss Sardana laughs and squeezes my arm. "Thank you for doing this, Effie. I'm just sorry no one thought to do it sooner. Sometimes we grown-ups get used to the way things are, but I promise, from now on, that will be different. I'll support you however I can."

"Thank you," I manage. Miss Sardana disappears into the crowd, which is still growing.

"OK, Effie." Angelika appears. "I think you'd better make a speech."

"What, now?" I ask, suddenly panicked.

"Before we get started, don't you think?" she asks. "Someone brought that big crate for you to stand on."

"Oh, OK," I say, trying to remain calm. "Great." I pick my way through to the crate, trying to remind myself that speaking in public to big crowds like this is part of the job if you want to be in charge of things. The trouble is that just because you're a natural-born leader, it doesn't mean that you don't get nervous sometimes. Right now my palms are clammy and my knees are wobbling like jelly.

I clamber up on to the crate and suddenly the crowd looks even more enormous. All of them are looking at me, so many pairs of eyes swivelled in my direction. I clear my throat, noisily.

"Hey. . ." I start to say into the megaphone, but there's a screeching feedback sound. My mouth goes dry, and I can feel my fingers tremble.

I don't know if I can do this.

CHAPTER *Thirty-Eight*

"Wooooo! Effie!!!" I hear a small voice yell from the crowd, and it's Zo, grinning at me, and then more people join in, and soon there are lots of people cheering.

I smile back at her, feeling some of the nerves easing off a bit, and then I pull my shoulders back, stand up tall and use my biggest voice.

"Hello, everyone!" I say, and another cheer fills the air. "Thanks so much for coming here today to stand up for democracy, and to fight for the Green Deal. We're going to be taking part in a big river clean-up today, and I'm just so happy and excited that you're all here. This is about all of us coming together to stand for the environment, it's about demanding change right here and right now. And we're doing something today that shows we're serious about being a part of that change!" There is more cheering at this. I look out at the sea of faces and I know what I need to do. "This is about all of us. I don't want to stand here and give a big speech." I hold out the microphone. "It's your turn. We all have a voice. Let's use it."

There's a silence, and I stand holding out the megaphone.

Then Angelika steps forward. She grins at me and takes the megaphone.

"Some of us might be young," she says. "But we are the ones who are fighting for our future, we are the ones who will have to deal with the damage caused by climate change. Powerful people who should know better have chosen to sacrifice OUR futures, because of greed. And we are here to say that is NOT OK."

A wave of loud cheers fills the air as Kevin steps forward and takes the megaphone.

"We come together today to show that we will not stand by and watch, we will not cross our fingers and *hope for the best*, NO!" He pauses dramatically here, and I realize I'd never noticed what a great public speaker he is. "We are a movement!" he yells. "We can change things! Starting with the way we run *our* school, and the way we take care of *our* community. Small actions are *not* meaningless. Because all of those small actions will become a wave of change, that will turn the tide on this disaster."

There's another explosion of cheers here. The applause is going on longer now.

"I'm so glad you all came here today," Ruby says, stepping forward to take her turn. "It makes me feel hopeful. It shows that we are not going to quietly go away, that we are here and we are loud and we are going to keep making ourselves heard, over and over until we know that everyone is listening! Together we really can change the world!"

Whooping and cheering fills the air, and then others start to step forward from the crowd to talk about why they're here and what they believe in and their words are powerful and strong and it's a million times better than in my daydreams. I scramble down from the crate and my friends surround me, pulling me into a giant group hug and jumping up and down.

After that things pass in a bit of a blur. Some people pile into the minibus and various cars, while the rest of us head to the river on foot. We lead the march through the gates and along the path, over the hill and through the woodlands, which are coming alive now with signs of spring. Spirits are high. People are laughing and chanting together.

"We will choose, we will decide

We will fight to turn the tide

When our planet's under attack,

What do we do?

We stand up! We fight back!"

By the time we get to the river, some people are already there.

Specifically, Iris, who is sitting behind a table full of litter pickers and bin bags, and next to her is Yia-yia.

"You didn't think I'd miss it, did you?" Iris cackles, waving her sign in the air. "I just wish Lennon could have come too. Loves a good protest chant."

"This is my first protest," Yia-yia says, adjusting her sunglasses. "I must say it is most invigorating. What a thing to have done, Effie. You should be very proud." She looks over her shoulder, where my dad is reaching up into a tree with his litter picker. "Dimitri," she calls regally. "There is a KitKat wrapper to your left... No, your left ... your LEFT." She turns back to me. "It's exhausting work, all this clean-up business, but it does feel good."

Another car pulls up by the minibus and a familiar voice shouts from inside.

"Hey, Kostas," Aaron calls. "Have you got room for one more?"

I run over. His mum is sitting in the passenger seat. "He absolutely insisted, Effie," she says. "I've got to go and pick Lexie up from ballet, then we'll be back to help. Will you make sure he doesn't overdo it? If his dad finds out, he'll be dead meat."

"I will!" I promise. "He can help Yia-yia and Iris to supervise."

We say goodbye to Aaron's mum and I help him to hobble into a folding chair. Iris puts herself in charge of group morale, and she's having the time of her life, yelling into the megaphone.

"What do we want?" she cries.

"Clean air!" the crowd chants back.

"When do we want it?"

"NOW!"

"Looks like you got a good turnout," Aaron says, taking in the big, happy crowd.

"Yep," I agree. "It's been amazing. And you needn't worry about your presidency. From the size of the crowd who turned up to vote, I think you're safe."

"Thanks to you." Aaron smiles at me, and I feel my cheeks get a bit warm. "You did this, Effie. If we get the school to make all these changes it will be because of you." He pauses. "And when I'm back at school – which I will be very soon – I'm going to do more to help you."

Now I really am blushing. It's the nicest thing Aaron's ever said to me. It's one of the nicest things *anyone* has ever said to me. "Well, maybe one day I will be the school council president," I say.

"In about seven months, I reckon." Aaron grins. "I know I'll be voting for you."

I grin back at him, and in that moment I know for certain that I'll run again. I know that losing hasn't made me weaker. It's made me stronger. If I can run and lose and survive, then I can do ANYTHING. Just look at what we've achieved today. One setback should never mean giving up.

"Thanks, Davis," I say, getting to my feet.

"Hey! Effie!" I spin around and see Katie walking carefully towards me. She's holding a towering pile of pizza boxes.

"I dropped into the pizza place on my way." She

grins as she puts the pizza boxes on the table. "Turns out they had a giant order that no one collected. Some big pizza party that no one went to. I thought you might like these for the troops."

People swarm round enthusiastically, digging into the pizza. "Thanks, Katie," I say. "That's really cool of you."

She gives me the faintest wink. "Well, I wanted to do something. Given that you didn't use my recording."

I stare at her. "That was *you*," I whisper. "You got me the recording."

"What Matt was doing was SO wrong," Katie says. "All those lies, the things he was saying about you. I thought he was my friend, but I could NEVER be friends with someone who acted that way. I thought if I pretended we were still on good terms I'd be able to get some dirt on him and help you out. Looks like you didn't need it in the end."

I beam at her. "But I did need it!" I exclaim. "Knowing someone was on our side, that someone believed in us . . . I really needed that! Thank you."

Her cheeks turn a little bit pink. "All right, weirdo," she says, "don't make a huge deal out of it."

I feel like my heart is about to burst right out of

my chest. Still, this river's not going to clean itself. I grab my own pair of gloves and a litter picker. Time to get stuck in.

A little while later I take a break and enjoy the feeling of the sunshine on my face. There's a slice of pizza in my hand, Angelika's arm is round my waist, Ruby's is around my shoulder. Lil is holding hands with Zo and Katie.

I am not sure I've ever felt happier or more hopeful than I do in this moment, standing with my friends and family, using my voice for something I truly believe in.

We're part of something big. Bigger than us, bigger than this one protest. A change is coming.

And I'm so lucky to be a part of it. I feel like I'm exactly where I'm supposed to be.

Effie the troublemaker.

Effie the leader.

Effie the rebel.

THE END

READING *Questions:*

I hope you've enjoyed Effie's second adventure!
Like me, Effie enjoys asking a lot of questions, and
she also loves hearing lots of different points of
view. Here are a few questions about the book that
you might like to talk about with your
friends or teachers.

For a lot of the book the Highworth Grange
students seem to be on Matt's side. Why do you
think that is?

What ways could you make your household or
school more green?

If you have read the previous book in the series, in what ways do you think Effie and Aaron's relationship has changed? What have they learned that makes them able to work together more effectively?

Reread the newspaper article in chapter ten, and the school council meeting minutes in chapter eleven. Are these both balanced accounts of events, or are the writers of each piece making their own opinions apparent?

In Chapter Twenty-Nine, Effie hears a recording of Matt insulting the students of the school, but she decides not to make the information public. Do you agree with her that Matt has a right to speak privately, even if he's saying mean things? Or do you think the students have a right to know what he thinks of them?

Effie and her friends make a brilliant zine about the environment, but zines can be about absolutely anything. Why not think about making one yourself? What would it be about?

Acknowledgements

I am so grateful that I got the chance to revisit Effie, her friends and her family for another adventure. I really do love these books and I believe in their message of hope and belief in the future. With that in mind the first people I want to thank are the young activists – some of whom are mentioned in this story – who are out there fighting hard for a better world. I wish you didn't have to, but I'm so glad you are. I stand with you.

As always I have to thank my agent Louise Lamont and my editor Gen Herr. As ferociously on Effie's side as I am in all situations, you both helped this book to come alive, and reassured me that it was OK to write a book that was angry as well as funny. I am always grateful for any opportunity that we get to work together, and I know I'm so lucky to have you both.

To the whole team at Scholastic: thank you, thank you, thank you. You are the ones who make this whole thing possible. Thank you to Aimee Stewart and Mirelle Ortega for making the book SO beautiful and for making the ideas in my brain into something tangible and funny and gorgeous.

A huge, enormous, great big thank you to Blue Peter and to Meryl Fernandes, Joseph Coelho and Jean Menzies – when you shortlisted the first Effie book you helped it to reach so many readers and I'm more grateful to you for that than you can ever know.

Thank you to the fantastic librarians and teachers who made a huge amount of noise about Effie, including my friend Helen Emery (and her whole team for the incredible World Book Day door!!), Lucas Maxwell, Scott Evans, and Loll Kirby among many, many more.

Thanks as always to my family and friends for their love and support. Special thanks to my excellent husband – what a clever thing it was, to marry the best person in the world.

And thanks to you, whoever you are, reading this. Thank you for joining Effie on her journey. I hope it made you laugh, I hope it made you angry, I hope it made you hopeful.

LAURA WOOD

Effie THE REBEL

ILLUSTRATED BY MIRELLE ORTEGA

■SCHOLASTIC

ALSO BY
Laura Wood:

Poppy Pym and the Pharaoh's Curse
Poppy Pym and the Double Jinx
Poppy Pym and the Smuggler's Secret
Poppy Pym and the Beastly Blizzard

Vote for Effie